THE WHITE FRIAR

Alexander Kielmann pursued his nefarious activities with impunity . . . blackmail, burglary, even murder. At Scotland Yard there were suspicions, but no proof available. Then Kielmann received a letter: '*You have ruined lives, but death is waiting for you . . . Your associates will suffer . . . They will receive their just deserts, you yourself being reserved for the last. I am Death, and I enclose my card.*' A visiting card showed a drawing of a monk in a white habit and cowl. Who was the *White Friar*?

Books by Donald Stuart
in the Linford Mystery Library:

MIDNIGHT MURDER

DONALD STUART

THE WHITE FRIAR

Complete and Unabridged

LINFORD
Leicester

First published in Great Britain

First Linford Edition
published 2012

Copyright © 1935 by Gerald Verner
Copyright © 2012 by Chris Verner

British Library CIP Data

Stuart, Donald.
   The white friar.- -(Linford mystery library)
   1. Detective and mystery stories.
   2. Large type books.
   I. Title II. Series
   823.9'12–dc23

   ISBN 978–1–4448–1151–3

1

The Warning

Early one cold and foggy morning the Thames police took the body of a ragged and emaciated young man out of the river just below Blackfriars Bridge, and there was nothing in his pockets to establish his identity or supply the slightest clue to his murderer, for he had not died from drowning but had been shot squarely between the eyes.

At the inquest which followed in due course a jury of his fellow-countrymen returned a verdict of wilful murder against some person or persons unknown, and that was the end of a sordid tragedy, or so it seemed, for nobody came forward to identify the stranger, and he was eventually buried in a pauper's grave.

Mr. Alexander Kielmann read the brief paragraph reporting the inquest at breakfast one morning, and smiled — a smile that showed in his white, even teeth of which he was justly proud — and promptly forgot all about it. Mr. Kielmann possessed a convenient memory that never troubled him unless he wished it to do so. He could, had he not been so reticent, have put a name above that unknown grave, but reticence was one of Mr. Kielmann's strong points, a fact that had exasperated certain officials at Scotland Yard for several years, and almost driven them to distraction.

Mr. Kielmann was a big man with a smooth and unctuous manner. His large, white face was unlined, and his eyes peered out from the little rolls of fat, which surrounded them with a benevolent and kindly expression that seemed to vouch for the goodness of Mr. Kielmann's nature.

'Dude' Dawson, Patricia York, 'Slick' Morley, and one or two others of his intimate friends had seen those eyes when they were anything but kindly. But naturally they kept this knowledge to themselves. Not out of regard for Mr. Kielmann's feelings, but because that smooth and slow-speaking man had a quick way of dealing with people who offended him. They remembered a nameless body that had been taken from the Thames.

Mr. Kielmann controlled a perfectly respectable company, which operated in textiles, and from which he and his associates contrived to draw a comfortable living. This was common knowledge to a section of the police force who had for years been watching Mr. Kielmann and his enterprises with great and increasing interest. What was not quite such common knowledge, but was certainly strongly suspected, was that Mr. Kielmann made larger sums of money from blackmail, disposing of stolen property, occasional judicious burglary, and in fact any and every form of crooked business that came his way, or could be side-tracked to divert money into his fat and greedy hands. This was, as has been said, strongly suspected by a few of the inhabitants in that grim building on the Thames Embankment whose duty it is to 'guard the children of the poor, and punish the wrongdoer'. But further than suspicion it never went, for Mr. Kielmann was a clever man, and took infinite pains to see that there was not a scrap of evidence against him, or any of those whose fortunes were bound up with his, by which he could be dragged before the law. Therefore, when the inquest on the unknown victim of an unknown murderer was over Mr. Kielmann merely smiled — which he did very readily — and proceeded to carry on his ordinary routine of business without, apparently, a care in the world.

He did this for a period of four months, and then one morning he had a rude and uncomfortable shock, for a new and alarming factor entered his life.

He received by the first post a typewritten envelope containing a letter and an enclosure. Both were conducive to filling his large being with vague and distinctly unpleasant feelings of alarm. The letter began without preliminary of any kind, and ran:

★　★　★

'You have broken hearts, and you have ruined lives, but death is waiting for you and those with you. Take heed. Each one of your associates will suffer in turn, and in proportion to the crimes they have committed. One by one they will receive their just deserts, you yourself being reserved for the last. I am Death, and I enclose my card.'

* * *

There was no signature, but on the plain visiting card that had been enclosed with the letter was a sketch in ink of a monk in white habit and cowl.

Mr. Kielmann frowned, and his smooth forehead wrinkled into a pucker. He had been the recipient of many anonymous letters, and all of them had found their way to the wastepaper basket without a second thought. But this was different. It gave him a nasty little creepy sensation in the region of his spine.

For no reason at all there rose before his eyes the vision of a white face, unshaven and haggard, its lips parted in a

5

grin of fear, and lank black hair from which the water dripped ... Mr. Kielmann shivered, and for the first time for many years, he ate no breakfast. That night messages went out to all his confrères, calling them to an extraordinary general meeting of the Amalgamated Textile Company, which in plain language meant that trouble was afoot.

They arrived at his well-appointed flat in Piccadilly shortly after eight o'clock, and took their places round the large table in Mr. Kielmann's rather ornate dining room, which had seen many meetings such as this.

When they were all assembled, the host from his seat at the head surveyed the company thoughtfully. Most of the principals who joined him in his nefarious schemes were there — 'Dude' Dawson immaculate as ever in a dress suit into which he appeared to have been poured in a liquid state, for no other explanation could account for its perfect fit; the stocky, red-faced prematurely grey Major Tison; the pale, colourless and almost emaciated 'Slick' Morley who looked as if he were dying of consumption and in reality possessed the strength of three ordinary men; the Frenchman Maurice, a tiny dark man with nervous twitchings to the muscles of his mouth, and Patricia York, with her flaxen hair and baby-face and carefully cultivated and permanent expression of open-mouthed wonder.

One face Mr. Kielmann sought for amongst that gathering and failed to find, and raising his eyebrows slightly, he looked at 'Dude' Dawson.

'Where is Arnott?' he asked in his gentle, purring voice.

'Don't know,' drawled Dawson with a rather bored shrug to his shoulders. 'Haven't seen him all day. He promised to drop into the club for tea, but never turned up.'

Mr. Kielmann scratched his many chins meditatively and looked up at the ceiling.

'Something must have detained him,' he murmured in a tone of annoyance. 'It's a great nuisance. Punctuality is the keystone of all success. I have endeavoured to impress that on you all during the time we have — er — worked together. It's a great nuisance. However, we will wait for a few minutes.'

He took a cigar from a box on the table, nipped off the end with a little gold cutter, and carefully lit it. Major Tison, sitting on his right, shifted impatiently.

'What was this call for?' he demanded at length as Mr. Kielmann puffed out clouds of smoke in silence. 'Have you something fresh on hand?'

His host removed the cigar from between his white teeth, regarded the lighted end deliberately, and then slowly turned his eyes upon the speaker.

'I have,' he answered softly, 'something — er — er — very fresh. We will, however, wait until our absent friend joins us. It will avoid repetition, which is equally abhorred by — er — artists and myself!'

He began to talk about a variety of subjects — current gossip, the relative attractions of various places of amusement, but as the time went on, the frown between his eyes grew deeper, and at last, when half an hour had gone by he suddenly stopped in the middle of the remark he was making to Patricia, and abruptly took out his watch.

'I really can't understand this,' he said shaking his head. 'I've never before known Arnott to be late for an appointment. Something must have happened to him.'

'Perhaps he never got the message,' suggested the girl.

'I telephoned myself this morning,' answered Mr. Kielmann heavily; 'so unless he is ill, there can be no excuse. Even then, he could have got his man to phone me here and say so.'

'Well we can't wait all night,' growled Tison. 'I've got an appointment at the Orpheum Theatre at ten.'

His host swung round towards him, and the benevolent expression had faded from his eyes being replaced by a hard glitter.

'I don't care if you've got fifty appointments!' he snarled harshly, 'you'll stop here until I tell you that you can go. You understand?'

Major Tison tried to stare out that hard gaze, but he was the first to drop his eyes.

'Of course, if it's important — ' he began with a conciliatory gesture, and the other stopped him.

'It is, most important,' he said and his voice had returned to its usual purring tone. 'I'm not in the habit of calling you all here except for something urgent.'

He looked across at the immaculate Dawson, who was smoking a cigarette listlessly.

'Go along to the study and ring up Arnott's flat,' he ordered. 'They may be able to tell you something.'

The younger man nodded, rose leisurely and deliberately crushed out his cigarette in the ashtray.

'All right,' he yawned, and strolled to the door.

They waited in silence after he had gone, each occupied with his own thoughts, and to judge from the slight moisture on Mr. Kielmann's forehead, and the way he kept twisting the butt of his cigar between his fat, well-kept fingers, his were not of the most pleasant.

In five minutes 'Dude' Dawson came back.

'Arnott went out at three o'clock this afternoon, and hasn't been back since,' he announced, lounging over to the table and dropping back into his chair.

'Did you ask where he was going?' enquired Mr. Kielmann.

Dawson nodded.

'Yes,' he replied, 'but they couldn't tell me. Page said he had a phone message, and left hurriedly.'

The fat man frowned.

'Had a phone message, and left hurriedly,' he repeated uneasily. 'I can't understand it, I can't understand it at all.'

He chewed on the end of his cigar for a few minutes in thought, and then removing it from his mouth laid it carefully on the big brass tray in front of him.

'Well, I suppose we shall have to get on without him,' he said with a laugh, and took an envelope from his breast pocket. 'The reason I called you together tonight was on account of this.'

He withdrew the letter and the card and passed them across to 'Dude' Dawson.

'I received that by the first post this morning,' he went on impressively. 'Have any of you had anything like it as well?'

Dawson read the letter with narrowed eyes, and looked at the card.

'I haven't,' he remarked. 'What does it mean? This is an ordinary visiting card, with a drawing of a monk or a friar on it.'

'I can see that for myself,' broke in Mr. Kielmann impatiently, 'and as to what it means, I don't know. Pass it on to Maurice.'

Slowly the letter and card went round until they had completed the circuit of the table, but each of the five people present shook their heads, and denied having had anything similar.

'I appear to have been the chosen one,' said Mr. Kielmann lightly. 'Now the question is, what is it all about? Is it a joke, or is it serious?'

'I should say it was a joke.' The little Frenchman spoke for the first time. 'Perhaps one of the people we have been — er — negotiating with is trying to frighten us.'

'That's my opinion, too,' declared

'Slick' Morley. 'Old Maynell probably. He kicked like the deuce at having to pay a hundred thousand for that marriage certificate, and threatened all sorts of things.'

Mr. Kielmaim shook his large head slowly.

'I don't think it's a joke,' he declared, 'and I don't think it's got anything to do with old Maynell.'

'Then who do you think sent it?' asked the girl with wide eyes. 'What does it mean?'

Again the stout man shook his head.

'I haven't the least idea who sent it,' he replied, 'but I think it means trouble.'

'Dude' Dawson laughed,

'Nonsense!' he said shrugging his shoulders. 'Just some silly fool we've got the better of, trying to get one back on us. Forget all about it, and tear it up.'

'Oh, you think that, do you?' Mr. Kielmann raised his eyebrows. 'Have you forgotten Len Sutton?'

Dawson looked at him, and his face went white.

'Len Sutton?' he muttered. 'Yes, I had

forgotten him. But he's dead You — '

'He's dead,' interrupted Mr. Kielmann, 'and he was sketching on an old piece of paper when he died. The sketch he was making when the bullet hit him was that of a robed monk!'

An intense silence followed his softly-spoken words and five faces suddenly stricken white and haggard stared fearfully at their chief. And then, like the snapping of a thread, the tension was broken by the shrill peal of a bell.

'That's Arnott,' said Mr. Kielmann. 'Go and see one of you. I've sent the servants to the pictures.'

'Slick' Morley was nearest the door, and he rose and went out. They heard him cross the hall; heard the click of the latch as he opened the front door, and then a little exclamation of astonishment.

'What's the matter?' grunted Major Tison. 'I wonder what — '

Morley's voice calling stopped him completing the sentence.

'Kielmann, come here, will you?'

The stout man rose quickly and with the others following at his heels, went out

14

into the spacious, well-lit vestibule.

'What is it, 'Slick'?' he asked, and Morley turned still holding the door open in his hand.

'Have you ordered a trunk?' he said with a puzzled frown.

'A trunk?' repeated Kielmann in amazement. 'No, why?'

'Well there was nobody here when I opened the door,' replied Morley, 'only that.'

He pointed to a large trunk that stood on the threshold.

Mr. Kielmann bent down and looked at it. Two leather straps encircled it, and attached to one of these was a label bearing the typeritten inscription: *Alexander Kielmann, Esq. With compliments.*

'That's damned funny,' said the stout man perplexedly. 'There must be some mistake. I don't know anything about it.'

'Better see what's inside,' suggested the bored voice of 'Dude' Dawson. 'Perhaps it's a present from an unknown admirer.' He chuckled.

'Let's get it into the hall, and open it,' said Major Tison, and seizing one of the handles he tugged hard. 'By Jove, it's heavy! Give me a hand, 'Slick'.'

Morley stooped down, and between them they succeeded in dragging the trunk into the lobby.

'Now for Pandora's box,' chuckled Dawson, and swiftly unbuckling the two straps he flung back the lid with a laugh.

The next second it died in his throat as he glimpsed the contents. With a little choking cry of horror he staggered back.

'My God!' he gasped, pale to the lips.

Mr. Kielmann gazed at the doubled-up form inside the trunk, and his mouth trembled as though with an ague.

'Arnott!' he mumbled incoherently. 'Arnott!'

'There's something devilish about this,' said Major Tison, the most collected of them all. 'Look here!'

He took a stained card that rested on the top of that crumpled figure, and glancing at it, handed it to Kielmann. The fat man took it in a trembling hand. On it was the drawing of the white robed monk, and neatly typed across were the words:

'*I am Death. To each of you I shall come in turn.*'

'Good God!' muttered Kielmann in a

husky whisper. 'What does it mean?'

They looked at each other with stark fear shining in their eyes, but no one could answer him, and then with a little moan, Patricia York sank fainting to the floor.

2

Mr. Kielmann Pays A Visit

Lionel Crane poured himself out a third cup of coffee, drank it slowly, and rising from the breakfast table crossed over to the mantelpiece and began with infinite care to fill his first pipe of the day.

Harry Pollard, his friend and partner, buttering the last remaining piece of toast, looked up from the newspaper he was reading.

'Did you see this, Li?' he asked. 'One of the directors of Kielmann's company was murdered last night, and his body left at Kielmann's flat in a trunk.'

'Yes, I saw it,' Crane nodded and applied a lighted match to the large bowl of his pipe, and drew one or two preliminary puffs with the enjoyment of a connoisseur.

'It seems rather mysterious, doesn't it?' his friend continued. 'Particularly the drawing on the card.'

'It is mysterious,' agreed Crane, 'but I can't say that I'm exactly surprised. The wonder to me is that something of the sort hasn't happened before. Kielmann's one of the worst scoundrels in London, and has been responsible for more suicides and wrecked lives than any other living man. I should think one of his innumerable victims has probably plucked up sufficient courage to turn round on him, and his rascally associates at last.'

'But why the drawing on the card?' inquired Pollard helping himself to more marmalade.

Crane shrugged his shoulders.

'Ask me something easier, old man,' he said going over to his desk and pushing up the top. 'Probably Kielmann could tell you.'

'According to this account,' said Harry, 'he hasn't the least idea.'

'Did he say so?' His friend seated himself in his swing chair, and began opening the morning mail.

'Yes, it was the first thing the police asked him,' answered Pollard speaking with difficulty on account of a large mouthful of toast and marmalade.

'Then I should think it's almost certain that he does know,' declared Crane drily. 'Kielmann must have become so proficient in the art of lying by now, that it's doubtful if he could speak the truth except by sheer accident. Kielmann is very careful to avoid accidents, that's why he lives in Piccadilly instead of Dartmoor!'

'I'm surprised the police haven't had him before now,' grunted Pollard.

'It hasn't been for lack of trying,' said Crane. 'For nearly five years they've been doing their best to trip up Mr. Alexander Kielmann, but he's proved too clever for them. He's the only criminal I've ever met who works entirely on a business-like basis. The whole of Scotland Yard, from the Chief-Commissioner down, knows that he's a crook, but they're powerless to do anything because they've never been able to get hold of a shred of evidence to warrant his arrest. Alexander Kielmann is beyond reach of the law at present, and will remain so until he makes a slip.'

He went on opening his letters, and a silence fell. Lionel Crane occupied a unique position. He was not exactly a private detective, neither was he an official one, but a combination of both. He was very friendly with Scotland Yard and the Foreign Office, and had done a considerable amount of work for each.

He had no interest whatever in the usual cases which come the way of the private investigator. Divorce and such like unsavoury public washing of linen were matters that he left to his lesser confréres. He possessed no office, and no clue to his profession appeared upon the plain brass plate attached to the door of his comfortable flat in Welbeck Street.

He was a pleasant-faced man of medium height, rather red-cheeked, and more than a little bald.

Harry Pollard was much younger. He was Crane's junior by nearly fifteen years, and in contrast to his friend, was tall and dark, with a complexion that was almost southern in its duskiness.

When Crane had first met him he had been a reporter on a Fleet Street newspaper. The friendship had ripened rapidly, and when Crane had suggested that he should leave his job and go into partnership with him, Pollard had leaped at the chance. For over six years they had worked together, and during that time had heard many strange stories, and taken part in many strange adventures.

Harry finished his breakfast, rose to his feet, dusted the crumbs from his knees, and walked over to the window.

'Is there anything special today?' he asked after standing for some time looking out into the street.

Crane shook his head.

'No,' he replied. 'It looks as if it were going to be a blank one. I shall go along to the British Museum and have a look at those Egyptian tablets they've just acquired. They are by far the most interesting relics yet dis — '

He broke off as there came a tap at the door, and Linker, his manservant, came in, carrying a card on a salver.

'There's a gentleman, sir, who wishes to see you,' said the man.

'Who is it?' asked Crane.

The servant extended the salver, and Lionel picked up the piece of pasteboard that lay on it.

Glancing at the name inscribed on the shiny surface, he uttered a little exclamation of surprise.

'Er — ask the — er — the gentleman to come up,' he said, and when Linker had taken his departure, 'What a nerve the man's got!'

'Who are you talking about, Li?' inquired Pollard curiously.

'Kielmann,' answered Crane.

'Kielmann?' exclaimed his friend. 'You don't mean he's called to see you?'

'I do,' assented Lionel. 'I'll wager it's about what occurred last night. Can you beat the consummate cheek of the man?'

Harry had opened his mouth to reply when Linker appeared again and ushered in the stout, smiling figure of Mr. Alexander Kielmann.

'Good morning, Mr. Crane,' he said with a great display of teeth. 'It was indeed kind of you to spare a portion of your time to see me. I am most grateful.'

'Please sit down,' said Lionel a little

23

coldly and ignoring the other's out-stretched hand. 'I presume you wish to see me about the regrettable affair that took place at your flat last night.'

'Exactly.' Mr. Kielmann deposited his hat and yellow gloves on the table, hitched up his immaculate grey trousers, and seated himself in the chair Crane had indicated.

His fat face was of an unhealthy pallor, there were dark circles round his small, beady eyes. His smile was unquenchable, and his white teeth gleamed pleasantly like chalked cliffs from a grey sea. He evidently expected Lionel to say some-thing, but the other remained silent and waiting.

'You have no doubt read the account in the paper concerning the murder of my poor friend, Arnott,' he began after a rather awkward interval.

Crane nodded.

'It was a dreadful thing — ghastly!' Mr. Kielmann went on. 'A delightful fellow, Mr. Crane — a man who wouldn't have hurt a fly — killed in the prime of life for no reason at all.'

'Then the crime is unique,' said Lionel Crane, 'for in the whole of my experience I have never yet come across a motiveless murder.'

'When I said for no reason at all,' amended Mr. Kielmann cautiously, 'I should have said for no apparent reason. Arnott was a hardworking man, respected by all who knew him, and — '

'Then the murderer must have been a stranger,' interrupted Crane drily.

'The murderer is a stranger to all of us,' said Mr. Kielmann. 'I have come to you to ask you to exercise your undoubted cleverness, and discover who this — this monster is.'

No greater contrast could be imagined than that which was presented by the appearance of these two men. Mr. Kielmann with his sleek black hair parted in the centre of his large head, his small eyes almost hidden in the folds of flesh surrounding them, his smooth, flaccid cheeks and double chin, stood for cunning, remorseless, untiring — the cunning of the stalking tiger.

Lionel Crane was watching him with

dispassionate interest. He may have been secretly amused at the man's sheer audacity, but if he was his face betrayed no such emotion.

'I daresay, Mr. Crane,' his visitor said in his slow, rather ponderous way, 'that you think it extraordinary that I should come to you?'

'It is rather like the mouse coming to the cat,' said Lionel, smiling a little grimly.

''Give a dog a bad name and hang him',' quoted Mr. Kielmann. 'For years I have had to fight the unjust suspicions of the police.' He shook his head sorrowfully. 'You would scarcely believe it, Mr. Crane, but I have actually been followed by detectives.'

He looked at Crane with an expression of outraged innocence.

'I can more readily believe that, Mr. Kielmann,' said Lionel, 'because I was myself at one time one of the detectives who followed you.'

Mr. Kielmann's face depicted the utmost incredulity.

'Dear me,' he said, 'you astonish me.

26

Absolutely amaze me.' He clicked his teeth. 'I am surprised that a man of your intellect should have allowed himself to be led away by the same libellous statements that appear to have influenced the police.'

Crane looked at him steadily.

'Mr. Kielmann,' he said, 'you know as well as I do that behind those libellous statements, as you call them, is more than an element of truth. That, in fact, they are in every respect rather less the truth, than an exaggeration of it.'

'Can you prove that?' said the stout man quickly. 'Can anybody prove that?'

Lionel blew out a cloud of smoke and shook his head.

'No,' he admitted. 'I must confess that's just the difficulty. Up to the present you have been far too clever.'

Mr. Kielmann shrugged his broad shoulders.

'I'm afraid, Mr. Crane,' he replied, 'you give me credit for qualities which I do not possess. I am a business man, but beyond that — nothing more. When the police started taking an interest in my — er

— enterprises, I gave them every help. I allowed them access to all my books and documents, and I could do no more. Was it my fault that they found nothing? No, it was because there was nothing to find. All I want is justice. My life is an open book, open for the fullest inspection.'

He spread out his smooth white hands as though inviting an even closer inspection than had been before afforded. Crane made no reply. He knew that stories had been circulated about the Kielmann gang, and knew that they were true. He was well aware that this fat, slow-speaking man could command thousands of pounds, and that most of his enormous wealth had been attained by crooked dealings.

After a moment's silence he leaned forward slightly.

'I presume that you did not come to see me,' he said a little ironically, 'in order to get my sympathy over your alleged police persecution?'

Mr. Kielmann shook his head emphatically.

'No, certainly not, Mr. Crane,' he answered with engaging frankness. 'We all have our little burdens to bear in this life, and that is mine. What I came to see you for was to ask you to look into this matter of the murder of my poor friend, Arnott.'

'But surely the police are investigating the matter,' said Crane. 'I fail to see what I can do.'

Kielmann made a gesture signifying his contempt.

'The police!' he replied disparagingly. 'They have been notified, as you say, but I doubt if they will be of much use in this affair. I have an unknown enemy working against me, Mr. Crane, and I want you to find out who it is.'

'Working against you?' repeated the other raising his eyebrows.

'Yes, and all the people who are associated with me in my business,' declared the stout man.

He took a gold-mounted morocco-leather wallet from his pocket, and opened it. From one of the numerous compartments it contained, he withdrew a letter and a card, and handed them to Crane.

'I should like you to read that,' he said

impressively. 'I received both by the first post yesterday morning.'

Lionel took the letter and the card and glanced at them. As he read the epistle that had spoiled Mr. Kielmann's appetite for his breakfast his eyes narrowed slightly.

'Have you any idea who sent you this?' he asked.

'Not the remotest,' answered Mr. Kielmann candidly, 'but you see it contains no idle threat, for on the same evening Arnott, who was one of my closest friends as well as a director of my business, was murdered and a replica of that card was sent with his body.'

Crane read the letter through a second time and then handed it and the card back to the stout man.

'You have, I suppose, shown these to the police,' he said.

Mr. Kielmann nodded.

'Then I think you'd better leave the matter in their hands,' continued Lionel Crane shortly.

The stout man raised his eyebrows questioningly.

'Am I to understand by that remark

that you refuse to help me?' he enquired slowly.

'You are!' retorted Lionel. 'I have no sympathy with a murderer, Mr. Kielmann, but I have less with a blackmailer, and if this unknown person succeeds in wiping out you and your — er — er — business associates, I can only say that the world will be a better place in consequence.'

For a moment Kielmann's face flushed, and his eyes gleamed with fury. But he managed by a supreme effort to control his temper, and when he spoke it was in his usual silky tones, though there was a slight quiver in his voice that betrayed his emotion.

'Very well, Mr. Crane,' he said softly with a tremendous flash of white teeth, 'you have done me a great injustice, a very great injustice, but since you refuse to take up the matter, there is nothing more to be said.' He rose and picked up his hat and gloves. 'Good morning,' he said, and crossed to the door.

'Good morning, Mr. Kielmann,' answered Lionel, and as the stout man turned the handle: 'I will give you a word of advice. Up to now you have been lucky — don't try your luck too far!'

Kielmann paused, and looked back.

'What do you mean by that?' he asked.

'If your mysterious enemy, the White Friar, doesn't get you, it is quite possible that I may,' said Lionel pleasantly, 'and in either case the result would be the same.'

The stout man shook his head in bewilderment.

'I don't understand,' he said slowly.

'Think it over,' replied Crane. 'Murder in this country is a capital offence, so either way it would mean your death.'

The other drew in his breath with a sharp hiss and his flabby face went grey.

'I thought you'd understand — *that!*' said Lionel Crane. 'Good morning!'

And without another word Mr. Kielmann left the room.

3

The White Friar

The slanting rays of the setting sun were flooding the countryside with a golden light as the slim figure of a girl in a neat-fitting costume came walking swiftly up the lane from the direction of the village. She would have been beautiful in any surroundings, for Mary Rayland was one of those fortunate people who possess a clear white complexion coincident with almost pure red hair, and her long deep brown lashes overshadowed eyes which sometimes looked blue and sometimes black, but were in reality a rather rare shade of violet.

She was frowning as she walked quickly with the easy grace of perfect health, but her frown gave place to a smile of welcome as she rounded a bend in the narrow road, and came upon a young man sitting on a stile swinging his legs.

'Hello, Dick!' she called, and looking round at the sound of her voice he dropped lightly to the ground and came to meet her. 'Were you waiting for me?'

He nodded and removed the piece of grass he had been chewing from between his lips.

'Yes, I called at the house, but they told me you'd gone down to the village, so I thought I'd come part of the way to meet you.'

'That was nice of you, Dick.' As he dropped into step beside her, she eyed the tall figure approvingly. 'How's your uncle?'

Dick stiffened, frowned, and shook his head.

'Much the same,' he replied, and there was a vague note of trouble in his pleasant voice. 'It would do him good if he'd only get out more. I've told him so, but he won't listen to me. It isn't good for any man to spend his days locked up in a stuffy library.'

'He goes out sometimes,' said the girl. 'I saw him in the village the other day coming out of the post office.'

Her companion shrugged his broad shoulders.

'Oh yes, he goes out now and again,' he said, 'but I mean regular exercise. It would stop him brooding over — well you know what — if he mixed with more people, joined a club and all that sort of thing. It's not as if he were an old man, he's only fifty-five.'

She nodded in agreement, and they walked on in silence. Dick had told her the story of the tragedy that had blasted Charles Mortimer's life, and her heart was full of sympathy for the lonely, self-contained man who had drained so much of the cup of sorrow.

'I suppose he's never given up hope of finding his son,' she said presently as they emerged from the lane on to the Horsham road.

'Never,' answered Dick. 'He's spent thousands of pounds on enquiry agents' fees, and had him searched for in every country in the world without result. It's my belief the fellow's dead, but I haven't the heart to tell uncle that. I think it's only the hope he will find him one day keeps him alive.'

'It's rather sad,' murmured Mary softly;

'life plays some rotten tricks sometimes. What did the boy do?'

'Embezzled three thousand pounds from his employers, and disappeared,' answered the young man, 'and he's never been seen from that day to this. That was ten years ago. Coming on the top of the death of his wife, it was a knockout blow for poor Uncle Charles. He simply worshipped both of them, and has never been the same man since.'

They had reached the wide gates of the drive by now and Dick halted as the girl paused.

'Won't you come in and see father?' she asked, and he nodded with alacrity.

'Yes, as a matter of fact, I was hoping you'd ask me,' he said shamelessly, and she smiled.

They continued their way up the well-kept drive with its border of Plane trees, and presently rounding a bend came in sight of the house. It was a white stone villa, low and rambling and built in the shape of an L, and looked what it was — the house of a fairly wealthy man. The trim lawn with its border of rose trees just breaking into bud; the flaming flower-beds; the thick hedges, all bespoke an air of prosperity and peace. And yet there lurked in this house a concealed unrest, a gnawing canker of hopelessness, and despair, that was shortly to break forth into stark tragedy, real and potent.

A trim maid opened the door to them, and her face broke into a smile as she saw who it was that accompanied her mistress;

'Where is my father?' asked Mary as the girl closed the door.

'In his study, miss, I think,' answered the maid. 'He had his tea there.'

'Go into the drawing room, Dick,' said the girl, 'and I'll find father and tell him you're here.'

'There's no need to disturb him if he's busy,' said Dick hastily. 'I can put up with your company, if you can put up with mine.'

She laughed and a faint flush tinted her pale cheeks.

'All right,' she said, 'but I must take off my things and powder my nose. I'll come back to you in a minute.'

He watched her slim figure as she flitted up the stairs, and then turned and entered the room, the door of which was being held open for him by the smiling maid.

'Would you like anything, sir?' she asked pausing for a moment on the threshold.

'No thanks,' replied Dick, and with another smile the girl withdrew closing the door behind her.

He strolled across to the window and looked out in the gathering dusk of the garden. The sun had set in an angry bank of purple cloud, and a thin breeze had sprung up with unexpected suddenness, whining through the trees eerily.

For no reason that he could have put into words, Dick shivered and came back to the big settee in the centre of the room. He hoped sincerely that James Rayland would be too busy to spoil the chance of a téte-á-téte that presented itself with Mary, for he had a lot to say to that young lady, and without being unduly conceited he rather believed that she would be — well if not pleased to hear it, at least not averse.

He was still racking his brains for a suitable opening — he had already discarded at least a dozen — when the subject of his thoughts came in, and he turned.

'You'll have to put up with me after all,' she announced gaily, 'father is expecting a man to see him on business and says he will come in later. I hope it's nothing serious, he looks rather worried.'

'Whatever it is,' said Dick selfishly, 'the unknown visitor has earned my eternal gratitude.'

She glanced at him and her colour deepened.

'That's certainly complimentary to me,' she said, and her voice trembled slightly, 'but hardly fair to father. He's never been accused of being a bore before.'

'I'm not suggesting that he's one now,' broke in Dick hastily. 'There's a lot I want to say to you, Mary, and — well, I'm sure you'd rather I said it without an audience.'

She stooped and switched on the electric fire.

'Getting rather chilly, don't you think?'

she murmured making a not very successful effort to keep the conversation from a subject that in her inmost heart she was dying to hear.

'I don't know,' said Dick. 'I'm much too interested in you.'

In two strides he crossed to her side and took her hand.

'Mary,' he said huskily, 'I love you — I love you, darling!'

She looked up at him her eyes shining, and without another word he took her in his arms and kissed her. It was not the opening he had so carefully rehearsed, but then on these occasions it never is. It seemed to be equally satisfying to them both, however, for the next two minutes they forgot everything except each other, till they were brought suddenly to earth by the tragedy which was at that moment preparing to creep upon the house from out of the gathering darkness.

★   ★   ★

James Rayland paced restlessly up and down his study with long, nervous strides, his hands clasped behind his back, and his chin sunk dejectedly on his breast. He was a tall man with the thin features that sometimes go with good breeding, and his grey hair and short military moustache gave him, the appearance of a retired soldier. And this appearance did not lie, for he had at one time held a commission in the Guards, resigning when he had met and married the beautiful daughter of Timothy White, the Australian millionaire.

Pausing in his promenade up and down the comfortably furnished room, he looked at the clock. The man was late — this mysterious individual whose telephone message that morning had drained the blood from his face, and toppled his peaceful life in ruins about his head. Who the deuce was this fellow Kielmann, and how had he got hold of his information?

Rayland frowned and continued his pacing. Anyhow it was sufficient that he had, and at any cost his mouth must be kept shut. He did not care so much for himself, but there was Mary to be considered. He stopped in the midst of a stride, as the faint purr of the doorbell reached his ears. This must be the fellow at last — ten minutes late! Unpunctuality was almost a crime in the sight of James Rayland. He listened, heard the sound of the maid's feet crossing the hall, and a muttered conversation. Presently there came a tap at the door, and the maid entered carrying a card on a silver salver.

'There's a gentleman to see you, sir,' she announced. 'He said you were expecting him. I was to say it was with reference to the telephone conversation this morning.'

Rayland took the card, and looked at the name inscribed on it.

'Ask the — er — man to come in,' he said shortly, and the maid withdrew.

He kept the piece of pasteboard, twisting it about in his fingers, and watching the door.

After a slight pause the girl returned, and ushered into the study a short, rather stocky man with a red face that glowed from the action of the wind.

'Mr. Rayland?' murmured Major Tison

with a genial smile, and Rayland nodded.

Then when the door had closed:

'Now, Major Tison, will you kindly explain the meaning of this visit? I was expecting a man called Kielmann. It was he, I believe, who rang me up this morning.'

'Mr. Kielmann has unfortunately been detained on urgent business,' said Tison deprecatingly. 'He sent his apologies and hoped that you would excuse him.'

'His detention has nothing to do with the police, I suppose?' said the elder man sarcastically.

Major Tison looked shocked.

'Dear me, no,' he said, 'Mr. Kielmann is detained on business, he has nothing whatever to do with the police.'

'I can quite believe that,' retorted Rayland dryly, 'but I should imagine that they will have something to do with him in the very near future.'

The red-faced man shook his head.

'I fail to understand you,' he said gently. 'Mr. Kielmann is a highly-respected business man. I am, myself, a co-director of the Amalgamated Textile

Company, and — '

'That's sufficient in itself to vouch for his dishonesty,' snapped Rayland. 'Now, Major Tison, let us cease this beating about the bush and come to business. According to the telephone message I received this morning, Mr. Kielmann has in his possession a cheque for two hundred pounds drawn twenty years ago in my favour, and signed by Lord Ardington. He alleges that this cheque is a forgery. Well it's useless to deny it, it is. The money has, however, since been refunded anonymously to Ardington, so what exactly is the position — blackmail?'

Major Tison held up a protesting hand, and his expression was one of positive pain.

'Really I beg of you, Mr. Rayland,' he murmured, 'Blackmail is a very ugly word.'

'It's a very ugly business,' grunted Rayland.

'I'm sure Mr. Kielmann would be the first to agree with you,' the red-faced man continued. 'Twenty years ago you contracted some gambling debts in the regiment in which you held the position of lieutenant. In order to discharge these, you forged the name of your friend, Ardington, to a cheque, You were never suspected — the suspicion fell upon Ardington's manservant whom you got to cash the cheque for you, and when he appealed to you, you denied all knowledge of it. He was discharged, but because he had been in the family for many years, Ardington refused to prosecute. I think briefly that is the story, isn't it?'

Rayland, groaned, and sank into a chair covering his face with his hands.

'I don't know how you got hold of the facts,' he muttered. 'But I have since made reparation both to Ardington and to Lane, and I can assure you that I have never ceased to regret that one lapse from honesty all my life.'

'Very properly — very properly,' said Major Tison virtuously. 'I am sure both Mr. Kielmann and myself appreciate your feelings. In short, when this cheque and the proof of your — er — little mistake came into his possession my friend and partner said that the right thing to do was to communicate with you at once as undoubtedly you would like to have the cheque, and er — er — to have it destroyed in order to save the unpleasantness which would occur if the true facts ever reached the ears of Lord Ardington.'

The elder man raised a haggard face, and looked at Tison steadily.

'Do I understand that you are prepared to hand over the cheque and whatever proofs you possess?' he enquired.

'Most certainly,' replied the red-faced man quickly. 'That is the object of my visit.'

A look of relief crossed the white face of the other.

'I am sorry — I'm afraid I have misjudged you,' he said. 'I thought that — this was' — he hesitated — 'blackmail.'

Major Tison shook his head, raising his rather bushy eyebrows,

'Put such a thought out of your mind at once, sir,' he declared emphatically. 'My friend and I would never dream of such a thing. The very idea would be abhorrent to us.' He paused. 'Of course, we shall expect something for our time and expense, but that is all.'

'I shall be most happy to reimburse you for any expense you may have incurred,' said Rayland going over to his writing table, and pulling open a drawer. 'If you will name what you think is an adequate sum,' he took out a cheque-book and laid it on the blotting-pad. 'And I need hardly add that this matter will remain as a secret between us?'

'My dear sir, you can absolutely rely on the discretion of Mr. Kielmann and myself,' answered Tison. 'I have here all necessary documents which I shall be pleased to give into your keeping.'

He took an envelope from his pocket, and Rayland stretched out his hand.

'There is just a little matter of — er — er — expenses and loss of time to be settled first,' continued the red-faced man with a genial smile. 'A mere detail, but I'm a business man.'

'Yes, yes, of course,' said Rayland hurriedly and opening his cheque-book he selected a pen from the tray in front of him. 'For how much shall I make this out?'

Major Tison screwed up his eyes, and gazed at the ceiling.

'Shall we say forty thousand pounds?' he murmured gently.

Rayland looked up and his face hardened.

'You rate your time very highly,' he said sarcastically. 'So it's blackmail after all, eh?'

Major Tison's smile broadened.

'By no means,' he replied. 'The forty thousand pounds is in payment for a block of shares in the Tulanga Oil Company, which Mr. Kielmann thought you would like transferred to you. I have them, together with the transfer papers which you can sign as soon as you have paid over your cheque.'

'I see.' James Rayland eyed his visitor keenly. 'The Tulanga Oil Company is almost a bankrupt concern, and the shares are not worth the paper they are printed on. But I suppose if anything came out, you and this man Kielmann would produce the transfer document, and it would let you out. Very clever indeed.'

'Don't you think we are wasting time?' suggested Major Tison. 'It is getting late, and I have a rather urgent appointment in London.'

'Which you will never keep,' said a hollow voice, and with an oath Tison swung round, his hand flying to his hip-pocket.

Framed in the open French window stood a figure, tall and menacing. It was clad in a long white habit that reached to the heels, and a cowl completely concealed the face save for two slits from which a pair of eyes glittered brightly. In its white gloved right hand it held an ugly automatic levelled directly at the red-faced man's heart. Tison felt his blood go cold as he surveyed the sinister form.

'Put up your hands,' said the newcomer in that dreadful toneless voice, and the blackmailer obeyed.

'Who — who are you?' he stammered with chattering teeth, and the other laughed, a shrill, discordant laugh without a vestige of mirth.

'I am Death!' said the voice. 'Arnott's met me. You will all meet me — 'Dude'

Dawson, Maurice, Patricia York, 'Slick' Morley, and lastly Kielmann.'

'What do you want?' Tison's voice was a hoarse croak and his throat was dry with the fear that had come over him.

'I want — you,' said the figure of the White Friar. 'You've never met death have you? Well, meet him now!'

The long-barrelled pistol cracked once, twice, and a third time, and with a choking sob, Major Tison collapsed in a heap on the floor, his life's blood crimsoning the white expanse of his shirtfront.

4

The Clue of the Handkerchief

The telephone bell in Lionel Crane's quiet study shrilled insistently, and with an exclamation of annoyance Crane laid aside the book he was reading and crossed to the instrument.

A gruff voice came over the wire as he placed the receiver to his ear, and he recognized it as belonging to Detective-Inspector Herrick of Scotland Yard.

'Hello Mr. Crane — that you?' asked the voice quickly. 'Listen. There's been another of those Friar murders.'

Lionel gave a little start and into his eyes crept a light of interest.

'I've just had the news by phone from Horsham,' the inspector continued rapidly. 'The local police rang through. It's Tison this time. He was shot at the house of a Mr. Rayland, and the murderer left behind him the card with the drawing of the Friar. Whoever is at the bottom of this seems to be making a speciality of Kielmann's friends. I'm going there now, and the Assistant-Commissioner asked me if I could get in touch with you, and suggest that you help us in the matter.'

'I'd like to,' said Crane quickly. 'There's something about these crimes that interests me. Where can I pick you up, and we can go down in my car?'

'Can you meet me at the Whitehall entrance to the Yard in ten minutes?' asked Herrick.

'Yes, easily,' replied Lionel.

'Good, then I'll be there waiting for you,' said the inspector.

Crane hung up the receiver, and as he turned from the telephone Pollard entered the room.

'We've got a job,' said Lionel. 'You might slip round to the garage and fetch the car. We're picking up Herrick and going to Horsham.'

In a few brief sentences he explained the gist of the Scotland Yard man's call, and Harry hurried away with alacrity, his eyes alight at the prospect of taking an active part in the Kielmann business, for the little he knew of it had interested him.

By the time the big car was at the kerb Lionel was waiting on the doorstep, and a few seconds later they were threading their way through the traffic in the direction of Westminster.

They arrived at the archway leading to the headquarters of the Metropolitan Police, with four minutes to spare, but the stout figure of the Detective-Inspector was already on the lookout, and he came up to the side of the car as it drew to a halt.

'Good of you to come, Mr. Crane,' he greeted, as he clambered in beside Lionel, and with scarcely a pause the car started off again. 'I've got very few more details than I've already given you, but I've given instructions that nothing is to be touched until we arrive. The fellow who shot Tison, however, was seen.'

Crane looked interested.

'Oh, he was seen, was he?' he murmured. 'Then you've got a description of him.'

Herrick grunted.

'Yes if you could call it a description,'

he said. According to Rayland's statement, and the local inspector, he was dressed in some kind of a white robe with a cowl attached that completely covered his head. It sounds to me like a bit out of a sensational novel.'

Crane smiled.

'So do quite a number of things that get into the newspapers,' he replied, 'but they're facts all the same. So this man, Rayland, saw the murderer, did he?'

'Yes, Tison was shot in his presence,' said the Scotland Yard man. 'You know, Mr. Crane, there's something deuced queer about this crime. First Arnott, and now Tison — particularly after the letter Kielmann received the other day. It was a typewritten affair and warned him that — '

'Yes, I know,' interrupted Lionel, 'I've seen it.'

Herrick raised his thick eyebrows in astonishment. 'When did you see it?' he demanded.

'Three days ago,' replied Crane. 'I had the honour of a visit from our friend, Kielmann on the morning after Arnott was murdered.'

He gave his friend the inspector a succinct account of the fat man's call at Welbeck Street, and how it had ended.

'What a nerve the man's got,' commented Herrick admiringly. 'I'd give ten years of my life to trap that man, Mr. Crane, and see him cosily locked up behind the bars in Cannon Row.'

'I think our mysterious friend who calls himself Death, and uses the drawing of a White Friar as his trademark will get him first,' replied Lionel thoughtfully. 'He doesn't waste much time. He's accounted for two of Kielmann's gang in less than a week. I wonder who will be the next.'

'Who do you think it can be, Mr. Crane?' asked the inspector after a slight pause.

'I haven't the least idea,' answered Lionel gazing absently at the flying countryside. 'I should say it was somebody whom Kielmann and his associates had grievously wronged, and who, finding that the police were powerless to touch them, has taken the law into his own hands.'

The Scotland Yard man rubbed at his bristly moustache.

'I can't say that I'm not rather in

sympathy with him myself,' he grunted. 'But of course I shall have to do my best to find him. The law is the law and a person can't go about killing people even if they are crooks.'

They lapsed into silence for the remainder of the journey, and it was nearly eleven o'clock when the car swung through the drive gates and presently came to a halt outside the trim, white house to which tragedy had come so suddenly and unexpectedly. It was blazing with light, and on the top of the steps leading up to the front door was the figure of a uniformed constable on guard.

He was evidently expecting them, for when Herrick gave his name, he saluted, and took them across the hall to a room at the far end in which they found a tall, rather thin man engaged in examining a pair of french windows that opened on to a broad terrace.

'Detective-Inspector Herrick?' he said questioningly as they entered, and at the burly inspector's nod: 'I'm glad to meet you, sir. My name is Weston — Inspector Weston.'

He shook hands, and Herrick introduced Crane at whom the local inspector looked interestedly.

'Very pleased to meet you, sir,' he said. 'I've heard of you, of course.'

'Is this the room where it happened?' asked Lionel as he noted the still form lying on the carpet in front of the writing table.

'Yes, sir,' said Weston, 'and except for the Divisional-Surgeon's examination nothing has been touched. I was very particular about that.'

Crane nodded, and crossing over, stood for a second or two looking down at the body.

'The murderer was evidently taking no chances,' he muttered. 'This fellow's been shot three times, and every bullet found a billet. That's worth noting.'

'Why?' asked Herrick quickly.

'Because it shows that he is fairly familiar with the use of a pistol,' replied Crane. 'In nine cases out of ten a person unused to an automatic would miss even at close range. The kick of the weapon has to be allowed for, and certainly the first two shots would go wide. The fact that all three hit the victim squarely in the chest argues that the killer was an expert in the use of a pistol.'

'Yes, that's quite true, sir,' agreed Weston, 'I never thought of that.'

Crane's eyes darted quickly about the room, and finally settled on the writing table. Stepping over to it he picked up the card that lay on the blotting pad and looked at it. 'This, I presume,' he said, turning to Weston, is the card the murderer left behind him.'

The local inspector nodded.

'And he came by way of the french windows?' It was more of a statement than a question, and again Weston nodded. 'Was no effort made to apprehend the man?' asked Crane.

'No. Mr. Rayland says that the whole thing happened so quickly, and he was so overcome with horror that before he could think clearly the murderer had vanished.'

'Yes, it must have been rather startling for Mr. Rayland,' said Lionel thoughtfully. 'Did you ask him what the dead man was doing there?'

'Yes,' replied Weston. 'He says that he had called to see him on a matter of business.'

Lionel pursed his lips and frowned.

'Before we go any further I should like to see Mr. Rayland and hear from his own lips an account of what occurred.'

'He's in the drawing room with his daughter,' said the local inspector. 'I'll fetch him.'

He left the room, and as soon as they were alone Crane turned to Herrick.

'I'm rather interested to learn what the business was that brought Major Tison to Horsham,' he said softly. 'So far as I am aware this man Rayland is not one of Kielmann's gang — and we pretty well know all the people who are intimately associated with that scoundrel — therefore he can only be one of their victims.'

'You mean they were blackmailing him?' asked the Scotland Yard man.

'Yes, or something similar. Rayland is obviously a fairly well-to-do man — this house and its appurtenances show that — and therefore well worth plucking.'

Herrick ran a stubby hand through his hair.

'If they've been trying to blackmail him,' he grunted, 'and we could make him talk, we've got 'em! That's all we want. We've been waiting for somebody to set up a squeal against Kielmann, but they never have and that's why he succeeded in keeping out of the dock all this time.'

'I doubt if even now you'll get Rayland to say anything against Kielmann,' said Crane shaking his head. 'Blackmailers are nearly always safe, unless they make a mistake in choosing their victims, for he can't give them away without implicating himself, and you can be sure that Kielmann is too wary to risk blackmailing the wrong person.'

He stopped and held up a warning finger as the door opened, to admit Rayland and the local inspector. The grey-haired man looked white and ill, and his hands trembled. Obviously the tragic death of his visitor had given him a shock that would take him some time from which to recover.

'You wish to see me?' he said dully as he entered the room.

'Yes, Mr. Rayland,' said Lionel gently, and pushed forward a chair. 'There are one or two questions we should like to ask you concerning what took place here earlier this evening. I am sorry under the circumstances to have to trouble you, but —'

'It is necessary, and I quite understand,' murmured Rayland, and sank rather wearily into the chair. 'What is it you want to know?'

'I should like you to tell us exactly what happened,' said Crane briefly.

The grey-haired man passed his hand across his forehead, and for a moment or two there was a silence. Then hesitantly he began in halting sentences to relate the arrival of Tison, and the sudden appearance of the white-robed figure through the window.

Crane listened until he had finished, and then:

'What happened after the shots were fired?' he asked.

'The figure took a card from under its robe,' said Rayland with a shudder, 'and

61

threw it down beside the — the body. Then with a horrible laugh it disappeared through the window.'

'Did you make no effort to stop it?' said Lionel.

James Rayland shook his head slowly.

'I'm afraid I was too dazed at the awfulness of the whole affair to move,' he confessed. 'It was so dreadfully sudden and unexpected.'

'What did you do eventually?' inquired Crane. 'The shots must have been heard by the rest of the household. Didn't someone come to find out what had happened?'

'Yes, my daughter did,' answered the grey-haired man. 'She was entertaining a friend in the drawing room, and she rushed along here at once. I had recovered a little by that time, and I told her that a man had been shot. She was horrified, naturally, and suggested telephoning to the police, which we did.'

'You say your daughter was entertaining a friend? Who was that?' asked Crane gazing steadily at the man before him.

'A Mr. Venner — Richard Venner,'

replied Rayland. 'He lives quite close to us.'

'I see,' Lionel's voice was a trifle absent. 'Was he still in the drawing room when the murder was committed?'

Rayland shook his head.

'No,' he answered. 'Mary — that's my daughter — said he'd been gone about ten minutes.'

Crane looked at Herrick.

'We'd better have a word with Mr. Venner. If he left ten minutes before the murder was committed, he may have seen something of the murderer. I suppose' — he turned again to Rayland — 'it was impossible for you to tell whether it was a man or a woman?'

'Quite,' was the reply, 'though I think it was a man.'

'Why?' the question came sharp and clear like the sudden shivering of a glass.

'Because I noticed the shoes he was wearing,' answered Rayland. 'They were big and heavy, a man's shoes without a doubt.'

'You were observant,' said Crane with a smile, and then changing the subject quickly: 'How long have you been acquainted with the dead man, Tison.'

'I've never met him before,' Rayland for the first time exhibited signs of uneasiness, which Crane's eyes did not fail to notice.

'As he was not a personal acquaintance of yours, Mr. Rayland,' he said, 'perhaps you would not mind telling us the reason for his visit. Sorry if I appear to be unduly curious, but I am sure you will realize that the more we know about the man, the more likely we are to light on a clue to his murderer.'

'Yes, yes. I quite appreciate your reasons for these questions.' Rayland's uneasiness was growing more apparent every moment. 'He came, as a matter of fact, to transfer to me some shares which he held.'

'Shares?' Lionel's eyebrows rose a trifle. 'Surely that's rather an unusual proceeding for a perfect stranger.'

'Yes — yes, it was.' The grey-haired man passed his tongue over his dry lips. 'But he had been recommended by a friend.'

'A friend of yours?' asked Crane.

'Yes.' The answer was almost inaudible.

'What was this friend's name?' Lionel went on. 'Perhaps he will be able to tell us something that will help the matter.'

'His name?' repeated Rayland. There was a long pause. 'His name is Alexander Kielmann.'

'Really!' the astonishment in Lionel Crane's voice was admirably assumed. 'I am surprised that Mr. Kielmann should be a friend of yours. His reputation is — well, not exactly the best.'

'So I believe,' an expression of discomfort crossed the face of Rayland. 'But — but one can't always — er — choose the people with whom one does business.'

'No, I appreciate that,' said Lionel, and there was a rather strained silence. 'Have you done much business with Mr. Kielmann?' he asked at length.

Rayland shook his head.

'No,' he stammered. 'In fact, this was the first.'

Crane raised his eyebrows.

'You were preparing to buy shares from a man with whom you'd done no business before?' he remarked incredulously. 'May I ask what the shares were which Kielmann was transferring to you?'

'Does it really matter?' muttered Rayland. 'Surely it can have nothing to do with the death of this man, Tison?'

'It may and it may not,' answered Crane, 'but we cannot afford to neglect anything that may throw a light on the identity of the murderer. I'm afraid I must press the point, Mr. Rayland.'

The grey-haired man shifted nervously about in his chair, and looked from Lionel to Herrick and back again.

'They were Tulanga Oils,' he murmured at last.

'Tulanga Oils?' repeated Lionel, and his eyes gleamed. 'Why, my dear sir, surely you must know that they are practically waste paper. The company is on the verge of liquidation.'

'Yes, I am aware of that fact,' answered the other.

'And yet you were prepared to buy them from Kielmann?'

Rayland nodded slowly.

'Mr. Rayland, I'd like to ask you a

question which I hope will not offend you,' said Crane quietly. 'Was Kielmann using any means to force you to buy these shares against your will?'

Rayland went pale to the lips, and his eyes dropped from the other's steady gaze, but he shook his head again.

'No,' he answered, 'I was going to take the risk entirely on my own account.

Lionel regarded him with narrowed eyes, then be shrugged his shoulders. He was convinced that Rayland was lying — that Kielmann had some hold over him that he had used to force him to buy these worthless shares — but if the man wouldn't speak, he couldn't make him.

'Had the deal been completed when Major Tison was shot?' he inquired presently.

'No,' said the grey-haired man wearily. 'I was just about to make out my cheque.'

'And you are prepared to swear,' said Crane, 'that you have no knowledge of the identity of the murderer, or the reason this man Tison should have been shot?'

'Yes, I'm prepared to swear to that,' retorted Rayland quickly, and there was something in his tone that made Lionel believe he was speaking the truth.

He looked across at Herrick questioningly, and the Scotland Yard man almost imperceptibly shook his head.

'I don't think we need detain you any longer, then, Mr. Rayland,' said Lionel, and the grey-haired man rose with obvious relief, 'I should, however, like to have a word or two with your daughter.'

'I will tell her.' Rayland crossed rather unsteadily to the door. 'I hope you won't keep her too long. Naturally this affair has upset her, and — '

'Of course,' agreed Lionel with a nod. 'There's no need, either, why she should be subjected to the ordeal of coming in here.' He glanced quickly at the sprawling figure by the writing table. 'If you would take us along to her, I think that perhaps would be best.'

'You go, Mr. Crane,' broke in Herrick. Inspector Weston and I will have a look round outside. The fellow may have left some kind of clue there.'

'All right,' assented Lionel Crane. 'You go with them, Harry, will you,' he added as Pollard, a hitherto silent spectator, looked at him enquiringly, 'and I'll join you after I've seen Miss Rayland.'

He found the girl sitting white-faced and anxious before the glowing radiator in the drawing room, and she looked round with a startled expression as they came in.

'This is Mr. Lionel Crane,' said her father gently. 'He wants to ask you some questions.'

'Please don't get up,' said Lionel as the girl was about to rise. 'I shan't disturb you for more than a few moments. Where were you when you heard the shot?'

'In here,' she answered in a low voice.

'Alone?' asked Crane and she nodded.

'Yes,' she said, 'I came back here after I had let Dick — er — Mr. Venner out.'

She reddened slightly, and Crane drew his own conclusions as to the position Dick Venner occupied in her life.

'How long had Mr. Venner been gone before you heard the shots?' he enquired.

Mary thought for a second before she replied.

'Between ten minutes and a quarter of an hour,' she said, 'certainly not longer.'

'Did you go straight to the study when the sound of the firing alarmed you?' he went on.

'Yes, I was terribly frightened,' she shuddered slightly. 'I was afraid something had happened to Daddy.'

'Why?' asked Crane quickly.

'Well, I knew he had someone with him,' answered Mary, 'and I didn't know who it was, and I thought — ' She hesitated. 'Well, I don't know what I thought, but I was humbly scared.' She smiled faintly.

'Naturally,' said Lionel. 'Now while you were in here with Mr. Venner, did you hear any sound — as though anyone was lurking about outside?'

She shook her head.

'No, nothing,' she said. 'But even if there had been anyone outside I don't think we should have heard it.'

Again the red mounted to her pale cheeks.

'We — we were engaged in rather an interesting conversation.'

'I see.' The corners of Lionel's mouth twitched slightly. He could guess the subject of the 'interesting conversation'. 'But after Mr. Venner had gone, did you hear anything then?'

'No,' she replied, 'nothing at all.'

'Where does Mr. Venner live?' began Lionel, and broke off as there came an impatient tap on the door, and Herrick entered hurriedly, his red face shining with excitement.

'I say, Mr. Crane, I've found something,' he jerked. 'It was lying between two of the pillars supporting the balustrade of the terrace.'

'What is it?' asked Lionel Crane eagerly, and crossed to the inspector's side.

Mary rose, and came over, too, as Herrick held out his hand disclosing a sodden handkerchief, of coloured silk.

'This,' said the Scotland Yard man, 'and it's got the initials worked in the corner.' He stabbed at it with a fat forefinger. 'Of course it may not be a clue at all, but unless there's someone in the house whose initials are R.V., I should say it was dropped by the murderer.'

'R.V.!' exclaimed Rayland. 'Good God,

it must belong to Dick Venner!'

There was a sudden silence, and then Lionel Crane sprang forward and caught Mary as she swayed!

5

Herrick Makes An Arrest

The girl had fainted, and carrying her limp form over to the settee, Lionel laid her gently down, and straightening up, turned to the anxious-faced Rayland.

'You'd better ring for some water, or better still, brandy,' he said crisply. 'It isn't anything very serious.'

The grey-haired man nodded, and crossing hurriedly to the fireplace pressed the bell-button.

'It's my fault,' he muttered penitently. 'I was a fool to say what I did.'

'It wasn't so much what you said, as the shock of finding the handkerchief at all,' said Lionel. 'Where does Mr. Richard Venner live?'

'The next house to this,' answered Rayland looking up from chafing the unconscious girl's wrists. 'Holmwood — it's about three hundred yards up the road.'

Crane nodded.

'I think we'll leave you to look after Miss Rayland,' he said, 'and go along and have a word with him.'

'Do you think Venner can have had anything do with — with this business?' asked the grey-haired man anxiously.

'I don't think anything at the moment,' replied Crane shortly. 'We will call back here after we've interviewed Mr. Venner,' he added as he crossed over to the door. 'Come on, Herrick.'

They left the drawing room as the frightened maid entered, and found Pollard waiting in the hall.

'The man who shot Tison came from across the lawn,' he said in a low voice as they came up to him. 'I found his tracks on the grass.'

'From across the lawn?' echoed Herrick in a puzzled voice. 'That's funny. This fellow Venner's nearest way would have been round by the drive.'

Crane smiled and raised his eyebrows.

'You're rather jumping to conclusions, old man, aren't you?' he murmured. 'We are by no means certain that Venner is the man we're after.'

'There seems to be a strong possibility that he is,' grunted the inspector. 'After all, we found his handkerchief practically outside the room where the crime was committed.'

'That proves nothing,' argued Lionel. 'It might have been dropped there on some previous occasion.'

'That's where you're wrong, Mr. Crane,' said Herrick triumphantly. 'It was dropped this evening, and quite late this evening, too.'

Crane shot him a keen glance.

'Oh, how do you make that out?' he asked.

'Because,' replied the Scotland Yard man, 'the space under the handkerchief was as wet as the surrounding stone, which shows that it was dropped after the rain had started to fall. And it didn't start raining until nearly seven-thirty — I asked Weston.'

Lionel frowned thoughtfully.

'That's a good piece of reasoning on your part, Herrick,' he said. 'But might not the rain have soaked through the silk?'

'It might, but it didn't,' was the repiy. 'You can see for yourself.' Herrick held out the square of coloured silk, which he still carried in his hand. 'Look, it's only damp where it rested on the wet stone and on the top — the centre is quite dry.'

Crane examined the handkerchief with interest.

'Yes, you're quite right,' he remarked after a short interval. 'This seems to be clear proof that it hasn't been lying there long.'

He handed the handkerchief back to the inspector.

'I think the best thing we can do is to go along and interview this man, Venner, without delay.'

'Do you want me to come with you?' asked Pollard eagerly.

'Yes, come along old man,' answered Lionel. 'There's nothing you can do here.'

A few seconds later the three of them were striding down the drive.

The rain had ceased, and a thin rind of moon cast a pale fitful glimmer over the countryside as they turned out of the gates and set off up the road.

'If Venner is the man who appeared at the window and killed Tison,' said Crane breaking a long silence, 'he must have worked pretty quickly.'

'Why?' asked the Scotland Yard man, 'He had plenty of time. According to all accounts, he left ten or fifteen minutes before the shot was fired.'

'Yes, that's all very well,' said Lionel, 'but the man Rayland saw was clad in a white robe. If it was Venner, where did he get that from?'

'He may have had it hidden in readiness somewhere close at hand,' suggested Pollard.

'Yes, that's possible, but it doesn't sound very likely to me,' replied Crane doubtfully.

'Anyway there's no getting away from the handkerchief,' grunted Herrick, 'there isn't a doubt that he was outside that window this evening. Practically at the very time the murder was committed. That's going to take a lot of explaining away.'

Crane nodded absently without answering, busy with his own thoughts. The finding of the handkerchief certainly seemed to point to Richard Venner as being the unknown killer, the mysterious being who called himself the White Friar, and who had apparently taken to himself the extermination of the Kielmann gang. But there were so many things against that solution that Lionel found it very difficult to believe it was the true one. There must be some other explanation for the presence of that incriminating piece of silk.

The voice of Pollard broke in upon his reverie, and caused him to look up sharply.

'I think this must be the place, Li,' said his friend, and Crane found that they had come upon a pair of wide gates set in a trim hedge. He saw the name painted in faded white lettering, and nodded.

'Yes, this is the house,' he said, and they turned into the winding drive.

The house, a large rambling building of ivy-covered red brick, and obviously much older than Rayland's residence, was in pitch darkness. There was not a light anywhere, which considering that it was nearly midnight was not surprising.

'Everyone seems to have gone to bed,'

muttered Herrick gazing up at the dark pile. 'We shall have to knock them up.'

He went up the steps to the front door, and searched in the dark for the bell. He was still searching, grumbling the while, when Crane drew his torch from his pocket, and assisted the inspector's efforts with a brilliant circle of white light. It revealed an old-fashioned, wrought-iron bell-pull, and the Scotland Yard man gave it a tug. They heard the jangled clang of a muffled bell somewhere in the interior of the house, and were preparing for a long wait when with startling suddenness a light flashed behind the stained glass transom, and the big double-doors were opened.

'Who's that?' asked a youthful voice sharply, and they saw silhouetted against the amber light from a shaded pendant, the figure of a young man.

He was fully dressed and held the smouldering stub of a cigarette in his hand.

'What do you want?' he went on looking swiftly from one to the other.

'I'm from Scotland Yard,' said Herrick

gruffly, 'and I've come over from Mr. Rayland's house. Are you Mr. Richard Venner by any chance?'

Dick nodded. Now that he could see more clearly, Crane thought that his face looked white and strained.

'Yes, I am,' he replied. 'Do you want to see me?'

'We should like to have a word or two with you,' said Lionel quietly before Herrick had time to reply. 'May we come in for a few minutes?'

'Certainly.' Dick held the door open wider and stood aside. 'I must ask you to be as quiet as possible. My uncle, who is practically an invalid, has gone to bed, and as he sleeps very badly I don't want him disturbed.'

He waited until they had all crossed the threshold, and then softly closed the door.

'If you will come in here,' he continued leading the way to a partly open door at the end of the big hall, 'we can talk.'

They found themselves in a small, comfortably furnished, but incredibly untidy room, which, judging from the photographs, and a large one in particular of Mary Rayland, was obviously Dick's own special sanctum.

'Now, gentlemen,' said the young man waving his hands towards a group of chairs, drawn up in front of the smouldering embers in the open grate, 'I shall be very glad to hear what it is you want to see me about. I must admit that it is a novelty for me to entertain people from Scotland Yard, though as you can see' — he indicated a well-filled bookcase — 'I am not unacquainted with their habits, or rather,' he added with a smile, 'such habits as are ascribed to them by several well-known authors.'

Although he spoke lightly there was an undercurrent of something very like fear in his voice, and Crane eyed him keenly as he replied:

'Surely, Mr. Venner, you can guess what it is that brings us here at this hour?'

'Since I am not a thought-reader,' answered Dick, 'I assure you that I can't. As you are all strangers to me, it can hardly be a social call, but beyond that I am afraid I must give it up.'

'Then you don't know what happened

at Mr. Rayland's this evening?' asked Herrick.

Dick's pale face went a shade paler.

'Happened at Mr. Rayland's?' he repeated with a badly-simulated expression of astonishment. 'No, I can't say that I do. What happened?'

He was lying. Of that Crane was convinced, and he was also a bad actor. Every moment, the tone of his voice, gave him away.

'Murder! That is what happened,' said Lionel gravely.

'Good God!' The young man's voice sounded husky as though his throat was dry. 'Who was murdered?'

'A man who had called to see Mr. Rayland on business,' replied Crane gazing at him steadily.

'How dreadful!' Dick dropped his eyes to the floor. 'Is Mary — er — Miss Rayland very much upset?'

'Naturally. It's been a great shock to everyone.' Crane was watching the spasmodic clasping and unclasping of the hands that rested on the arms of the chair. 'We came to see you, Mr. Venner, in the hope that you might be able to give us some information.'

'I? Information?' said Dick in a startled tone. 'What information can I give you? I — I knew nothing about it until you told me just now.'

'Then we appear to have had our visit for nothing,' replied Crane. 'We thought that as you only left the house a few minutes before the crime took place, you might have seen something of the murderer.'

'I saw no one,' declared the other quickly — too quickly Crane thought. 'I came straight home and never met a soul.'

'I see.' Lionel nodded, his brows wrinkled in a frown. 'Did you go by the main road, or did you take a short cut?'

'I went by the main road,' answered Dick.

'You didn't go near the terrace on to which the french windows of Mr. Rayland's study opens?' enquired Crane casually.

'No of course not. What should I have been doing there?' replied the young man.

'I went straight down the drive.'

'Then how do you account for the fact, Mr. Venner,' snapped Herrick suddenly, 'that we found this handkerchief of yours almost immediately outside the window?'

The blood receded from Dick's face, leaving it white to the lips, and into his eyes crept a hunted strained expression, as the inspector took the incriminating object from his pocket and held it out.

'I — I don't know,' he stammered passing his tongue over his dry lips. 'I may have dropped it on a previous visit yesterday, or the — day before.'

'That won't do,' said the Scotland Yard man grimly; 'We have ample evidence that it was dropped where we found it this evening — in fact, at the time the murder was committed.'

'Well, I know nothing about it,' said Dick hoarsely, and his forehead gleamed damp in the light. 'Good God, you don't think I killed the man, do you! I've never met Tison in my life — '

'How did you know his name was Tison?' broke in Crane sharply, and the other caught his breath.

'You mentioned it didn't you?' he asked, 'when you told me what had happened.'

'No names were mentioned at all,' answered Herrick sternly.

'Then I must have heard it — when he called to see Rayland,' said Dick sullenly, and then with a sudden outburst as he caught sight of the expression on Crane's face: 'What are you looking at me like that for? I tell you I know nothing about it — nothing about it at all.'

He rose to his feet, and began pacing the room with jerky uneven strides.

'Then perhaps you can offer an explanation of how this handkerchief got there?' growled Herrick.

'I can't — I've told you I can't. I don't know how it got there. All I know is, I didn't put it there.' A spark of colour had crept into his face, and his eyes glittered with a feverish light. 'Besides, if you think I killed this man, where do you suppose I got the white robe and pistol from? You surely don't imagine that I habitually carry such things with me. It — '

He broke off in confusion as he suddenly realized what he had said.

'Mr. Venner,' said Crane in a hard voice, 'why will you persist in lying to us?'

'Lying to you?' muttered Dick. 'I'm not. I'm telling you the truth.'

'You are not,' Lionel went on, interrupting him. 'You have stated that you knew nothing about this crime until we told you. And yet although neither of us mentioned the fact you are aware that the murderer was wearing a white robe, and also the name of the visitor. Come, why don't you make a clean breast of it, and tell us all you know.'

Dick stopped his pacing, and leaning against the back of a chair, pressed a shaking hand over his damp forehead.

'I've nothing to tell you,' he said stubbornly after a little pause, 'I know nothing about it.'

'Then I shall have to arrest you on suspicion,' jerked Herrick grimly. He went over and laid his hand on Dick's arm. 'And I may as well warn you now that anything you say may be used later as evidence.'

'But this is monstrous!' exclaimed the young man shaking his arm free from the inspector's hand. 'I'm as innocent as you are.'

'I'm afraid we shall have to leave that for a jury to decide,' retorted the Scotland Yard man, 'and I should advise you not to make a fuss. It will only go against you.'

Dick turned his drawn face appealingly towards Crane.

'Surely you don't think I'm guilty,' he asked and Lionel shrugged his shoulders.

'I must say,' he replied, 'that your behaviour is most peculiar, and you've certainly brought this on yourself. I fail to see under the circumstances what else Inspector Herrick can do. It's obviously his duty to detain you. If you're innocent you'll have ample opportunity of proving it. In the meanwhile I can only repeat the inspector's advice, and suggest that you take this as calmly as possible.'

Dick looked at him in silence, and his mouth set in a firm line.

'All right,' he said. 'I won't give any trouble. If you'll let me leave a note for my uncle, I am ready when you are, Inspector.'

It was nearly dawn when Crane and Pollard reached Welbeck Street, and throughout the journey back, Lionel had hardly spoken a word. With his chin sunk on his breast, and his eyes half-closed, he had been lost in thought oblivious to life, time and place, and when Harry brought the big car to a halt outside the flat, he had had to tap his friend on the shoulder to rouse him from his reverie. Weary both mentally and physically, Pollard had hastily swallowed a sandwich and a cup of coffee and had gone to bed, leaving Crane alone for a final pipe.

Lionel was far from satisfied with way things had turned out. Although the evidence was fairly black against Dick Venner, and Herrick could certainly have done nothing else coincident with his duty but arrest him, Crane found it difficult to believe that the young man was the unknown being who had pitted himself against the Kielmann gang, to believe it, he had also to believe that Venner was guilty of the murder of

Arnott, for both crimes were obviously the work of the same hand Although there was nothing impossible about such a belief, something in his brain rebelled against the idea.

After taking Venner to the local station and charging him, they had returned to the scene of the tragedy to find that Mary had gone to bed, a fact for which Lionel was grateful, for he guessed the tremendous shock it would give the girl when she heard of Dick's arrest. Rayland had been astounded at the news, and made no secret of the fact that he whole-heartedly believed in the young man's innocence. And to a certain extent, Crane was in agreement with him, though for the life of him he could not see why Venner should have lied, pretending that he knew nothing about the crime when from his own lips he betrayed the fact that he must have known all the time.

For nearly two hours Lionel sat on thinking over the whole business, but when at the sound of the clanking of milk-carts in the street outside, he finally rose and went to his bedroom, he had arrived at no definite conclusion, and had to admit to himself that the whole affair was one of the most mysterious businesses he had ever come up against.

And it was to prove even more mysterious by the morning, for at ten o'clock he was awakened from a heavy sleep by Linker who informed him that Inspector Herrick was waiting in the sitting room. Struggling into a dressing gown he found that weary official striding up and down in a state of great excitement.

'Mr. Crane,' he cried, as Lionel entered, 'we shall have to release Venner, he's not the man.'

Lionel Crane blinked at him, rubbing the sleep from his eyes.

'Why, what's happened?' he asked interestedly.

'This,' jerked the Scotland Yard man. 'I've just had a phone message from Horsham. At nine o'clock this morning Rayland was shot dead in the grounds of his house, and lying by the side of the body, was a visiting card, and on it was the rough drawing of a White Friar!'

6

A Shock for Mr. Kielmann

The birth of the gang of which Mr. Alexander Kielmann was the acknowledged head had neither been an accident, nor had it been intended to run on exactly the lines it subsequently followed.

The main structure — the hub so to speak, on which all other side issues revolved was Kielmann himself, with his extraordinary financial genius, and lightning exploitation of every advantage that came his way. Outwardly he was the managing director of the Amalgamated Textile Company, a purely business concern, which complied with the law, paid quite respectable dividends, and cloaked other less innocent operations which never appeared in the official records of the corporation.

The sidelines of the gang were numerous and extensive, for Mr. Kielmann had a fat finger in every unsavoury pie. The thief freshly discharged from jail did not openly ask the stout man for money with which to purchase a new kit of burglar's tools, but it eventually came out of his capacious pocket. The dope-dealers, requiring finance for a consignment of illicit drugs knew whom to approach for the necessary capital. The cardsharper who wanted money to work one of the big steamship lines could always get it from the same source.

Some of the people he financed were on the borderline of respectability, others frankly infamous. Nothing was too big, and nothing was too small for Mr. Kielmann's cosmopolitan interests, and the only thing that was common to all his many enterprises was that there must be a large profit for Mr. Kielmann to pocket. Unless this was inevitable, his coffers were tightly closed and remained so.

Yet in spite of all these irons in the fire Mr. Kielmann's name never appeared as being at the back of any of these undertakings. So cunning were the methods by which he worked that it is doubtful if he could have been traced behind any of the operations, which he virtually controlled.

Late on the morning following the shooting of Major Tison, Mr. Kielmann sat drinking coffee clad in a dressing gown in the sitting room of his Piccadilly flat. There were dark circles round his beady eyes, and the skin hung beneath in unhealthy pouches. His usually smooth face was unshaven, and of an intermediate colour between white and grey that was the reverse of pleasant to look upon.

The hand that held the cup shook so that he found it difficult to avoid spilling the contents, and the cause of his perturbation was not entirely traceable to the short paragraph concerning the death of his friend and associate that appeared in the morning's paper, which lay open on the floor. In a great measure it was due to a certain precaution which Mr. Kielmann had deemed it necessary to carry out, and which had sent him to Horsham in the small hours of the morning, a journey from which he had but recently returned.

'Slick' Morley had accompanied the

unfortunate Tison when the latter had paid his ill-fated visit to Rayland, waiting for him in the car which had brought them both from London, and which they had stopped, in a narrow lane a few hundred yards from the house. It had been Morley who had arrived at Kielmann's flat, white-faced and trembling in every limb to acquaint him in disjointed sentences of the tragedy that had occurred at Horsham. Mr. Kielmann had listened, his heart in his mouth, but it was not so much the unknown enemy who was working against him that he feared at that moment, but what James Rayland might in his panic reveal to the police. A word from him and Kielmann was ruined — ruined irretrievably — and as he sat through the long hours of the night thinking, there arose before his mental gaze the vision of a cold cell, and a gravel-paved exercise yard, and he shivered. At all costs this risk must be obviated, and there was only one way. Rayland must be silenced. It was six o'clock when Mr. Kielmann, enveloped in a heavy overcoat, made his way to his private garage, and took out his little two-seater coupe. It was a stroke of genius on his part which prompted him to take a train visiting card from his desk, and with infinite care draw on its blank surface the now familiar figure of the White Friar. Why should not the mysterious unknown get the credit for the crime he contemplated? He smiled mirthlessly as he set down his cup. The silencing of Rayland had been easier than he expected. It was sheer luck that had brought the man out on that morning stroll — sheer luck at least for Kielmann, for he had been racking his brains how with safety he could get at the man he sought. The dull 'plop' of the silenced pistol had been heard by nobody, and after leaving the card by the side of the body he had hurried to make his way back to the place where he had left his car, so far as he knew, unseen and unsuspected by a soul.

Rayland's death would, of course, be attributed by the police to the same hand that had shot Tison, and altogether it had been a very satisfactory and cleverly carried out morning's work.

Now, however, that the immediate danger had been accounted for, Mr. Kielmann's mind had reverted to the other and very real menace that emanated from the unknown person who called himself death, and whose existence was like a sword of Damocles over their heads. Who was he, and why was he taking to himself the role of avenger? It must be somebody whom Kielmann and his associates had deeply wronged. But there were so many that it was next to an impossible task to select the right person from the legion who had suffered at his hands.

He was still thinking the matter over when 'Dude' Dawson and Morley were announced. Dawson was as immaculate as ever, even to the white carnation in his buttonhole, but one glance at his drawn face convinced Kielmann that he had slept little that night.

'This is awful — ghastly!' he burst out as soon as the door had closed behind the servant who had admitted them, and it was noticeable that his usual drawl had completely disappeared. 'What are you going to do about it?'

'What am I going to do about what?' growled Mr. Kielmann looking at his friend and confrére with no very friendly eye.

'This horrible business of the death of Tison,' said Dawson helping himself to a cigarette with a shaking hand. 'We've got to do something, there's no knowing who may be the next.'

'Well, what do you suggest we do?' enquired the stout man sarcastically. 'Lock ourselves in a safe deposit? Because I'm telling you that that's about the only place where this fellow's not likely to get at us.'

'For God's sake stop joking!' snapped 'Slick' Morley irritably. He looked even thinner than usual. 'It's not funny, it's damned serious. First Arnott and now Tison, and we don't even know who's going to be the next on the list. The only thing we know for certain is that you're going to be the last.'

'I find some comfort in that,' said Mr. Kielmann, 'but at the same time I fail to see what we can do, except take precautions.'

'How can we take precautions when we don't know who's at the bottom of this business?' asked 'Dude' Dawson, drawing clouds of smoke into his lungs and exhaling them slowly. 'That's the first thing we've got to do — find out whom we're up against.'

Mr. Kielmann nodded.

'That's all very well,' he agreed, 'but how are you going to set about it?'

'I don't know — I've spent the whole night trying to think,' answered Dawson. 'I was hoping you'd be able to suggest a plan. Once we know the identity of this White Friar man, we shall be safe.'

Mr. Kielmann rose and began pacing the room, his hands in the pockets of his dressing gown:

'I'll tell you one thing,' he said after a moment's pause. 'Whoever he is, he's somebody who knows our business as well as we know it ourselves. Somebody who has, or has had access to our working methods.'

'You mean one of ourselves?' exclaimed Morley and the stout man nodded

'Rubbish!' broke in Dawson. 'You might as well say it is I, or Morley, or

98

Patricia, or Maurice.'

'Well, why not?' demanded Kielmann stopping suddenly. 'Why shouldn't it be any one of you?'

'Because none of us would have any motive — ' began Morley, and Mr. Kielmann interrupted him.

'Oh yes, you would,' he said. 'Have you forgotten our arrangement? If any of us dies or drops out, the remainder share the money we have accumulated equally amongst them, with the exception of a twenty per cent bonus which comes to me first. The last three years have been pretty good, with something like three hundred thousand in the general sum.'

There was a dead silence when he finished speaking. The possibility that the mysterious killer might be one of themselves had not occurred to them before.

'According to your theory, the most likely person would be yourself,' remarked 'Slick' Morley at length, a trifle unpleasantly, 'since you're supposed to be the last to remain alive.'

'Oh, what's the use of talking rubbish?' snarled 'Dude' Dawson impatiently. 'Of course, it's not one of ourselves who's working this stunt. It's somebody who's got a grudge against us. Instead of putting forward ridiculous suggestions, it would be better if we employed our time by trying to think out some of the most likely people.'

He flung himself into a chair and his forehead crinkled in thought.

'There's young Dillon, whom we caught for sixty thousand pounds — he swore he'd get even somehow.'

'He's in Africa,' said Kielmann shortly.

'And there's Fawcett,' went on Dawson without taking any notice of the interruption. 'He made a terrific fuss at the time, and there's Gould — '

'There are dozens,' snapped Mr. Kielmann, 'It's like looking for a needle in a haystack. Why don't you suggest Len Sutton, and be done with it?'

'Slick' Morley shivered and screwed up his eyes.

'For God's sake, don't mention Len Sutton!' he said quickly.

'Why not?' snarled Kielmann turning on him quickly. 'He's an example that keeps most of the smaller fry who do our dirty work from squealing. They remember what happened to him, and change their minds.'

'Talking of squealing,' said 'Dude' Dawson, 'What about Rayland? Suppose he starts saying — '

'Suppose nothing!' broke in the stout man. 'Rayland will have to put up a mighty loud squeal to reach from where he's gone.'

The two men caught the significance of his words, and their faces paled.

'You mean he's — ' said 'Slick' Morley in a whisper leaving the sentence unfinished.

'I mean he's dead,' replied Mr. Kielmann shortly. 'I was leaving nothing to chance.'

'When did it happen?' asked Dawson hoarsely. For neither he nor Morley were as hardened to crime as the stout man in the dressing gown.

'It happened this morning,' said Kielmann curtly. 'I had only got back a short time before you two arrived. For the love of Caesar, don't look so horrified!' he broke out angrily. 'It had to be done.'

'We agreed that there should be no more that sort of thing after the Sutton affair,' muttered Dawson uneasily. 'I don't like it — it — '

Kielmann swung round and striding up to his chair, thrust his large face close to the other's.

'Oh, you don't like it, don't you?' he grated, his small eyes flashing. 'You don't like it, eh? I suppose you'd prefer to spend ten years in Dartmoor, you white-livered dude! Let me tell you this — I don't care for your likes and dislikes. I'm head of this organisation, and I'm going to run it my way — see?'

The ferocity in his voice was extraordinary. No one who did not know him intimately would have suspected the mild, purring Mr. Kielmann capable of such malignancy.

'So don't let's hear any more of your likes and dislikes,' he said recovering some of his normal tone. 'I know what I'm doing.'

'There's no sense in us quarrelling,' said 'Slick' Morley pacifically. 'Although surely it was rather a risk to take with the house in the hands of the police.'

'The police!' Kielmann gave a contemptuous shrug and snapped his fingers. 'Since when have I been scared of a handful of flat-footed detectives? Besides they'll never suspect I had anything to do with it. I took the precaution of leaving one of our unknown friend's visiting cards beside the body.'

'The White Friar?' asked Dawson, and the stout man nodded.

'Yes, so they'll put it down to the same hand that shot Tison,' he said complacently. 'There's absolutely nothing to connect me with the affair at all, and — '

There was a knock at the door, and he broke off.

'Come in,' he said, and his manservant entered with a card.

'There's a gentleman wants to see you, sir,' he said, and Kielmann took the card from the salver and read the name.

'Lionel Crane!' he exclaimed for the moment startled. 'What's he come here for?'

'What's he want?' muttered 'Slick'

Morley in alarm.

Mr. Kielmann stopped him with a gesture.

'How do I know?' he snapped. 'He'll probably tell us himself, if we wait.'

He turned with a bland smile and flashing teeth as Crane was ushered in, and held out his hand.

'My dear Mr. Crane, what a pleasant surprise!' he said unctuously. 'To what am I indebted for the pleasure of this visit?'

Lionel ignored the fat white hand extended to him, and looked Mr. Kielmann straight in the eyes.

'I've called to know what you were doing at Horsham between seven and nine this morning,' he said crisply, and Alexander Kielmann's face went suddenly grey!

7

Another Victim

It was only for a moment that the stout man lost control over himself. The next second he had regained a grip of his nerves; but Crane had seen and made a mental note of that swift change of expression.

'My dear Mr. Crane,' he said with an admirable assumption of astonishment, 'I really don't know what you mean.'

'Perhaps I didn't speak quite clearly enough,' replied Lionel. 'I'm sorry. I had no idea that you suffered from deafness. I will repeat my question.' He raised his voice a trifle. 'I asked you, Mr. Kielmann, what you were doing at Horsham this morning at the time that James Rayland was shot in the grounds of his house?'

'I'm afraid you're still speaking in riddles,' said Mr. Kielmann shaking his head slowly. 'I have not been to Horsham either this morning, or any other morning, and your statement that Mr. James Rayland has been shot is news to me.'

'Yes, I'm sure it is,' answered Lionel, and there was no mistaking the sarcasm in his voice. 'I've no doubt that it is also news to you that you were seen on the Horsham road this morning at a few minutes after nine o'clock.'

It was pure bluff on his part, for he had no more definite information regarding Mr. Kielmann's presence in Horsham than that offered in the contents of the telegram which had arrived almost on the heels of Herrick, and which reposed at that moment in his jacket pocket. But he had been witness to the momentary expression of dismay that had crossed the fat man's face when he had snapped his question on entering, and he knew that the telegram did not lie.

'I assure you, Mr. Crane,' said Kielmann, 'that your information is incorrect. I have not left London. Both my friends here will bear out what I say.'

Crane looked from one to the other of

the two men who pale and visibly perturbed were standing near the fireplace.

'I'm afraid that even the sworn statements of both Mr. Dawson and Mr. Morley would hardly serve to convince me,' he remarked with a curl of his lips. 'They are neither of them noted for their veracity.'

'What do you mean?' growled 'Slick' Morley, his thin hatchet face hardening.

'What I say!' retorted Lionel, and deliberately ignoring Morley's muttered exclamation, he turned again to Kielmann. 'I believe that you were at Horsham this morning,' he said sternly, 'and I believe that you shot Rayland in order to prevent the possibility of his talking, afterwards leaving a card with a drawing of the White Friar beside the body, so that the police would think that the murder had been committed by the same hand that killed your confederate Major Tison.'

'I — ' began Mr. Kielmann, but Crane held up his hand and stopped him.

'Let me finish,' he went on and the words fell from his lips like slivers of ice.

'I know you, Kielmann, better than you imagine, and I know your methods and how you make your money, and I know just how much profit there is in that company of yours which makes such an admirable cloak for your other business. You can sue me for slander if you like, for what I am going to say is actionable, and if you do I shall be happy to fight the case. Somehow, however, I don't think you will. You are a blackmailer, a thief, a fence and possibly worse. Up to now you've been clever enough to cover your tracks. I don't mind admitting that there is not a tittle of evidence against you. But I know that what I am accusing you of is true, and so do the police, and a great number of other people whose lives you have ruined and broken. I know why Lady Northwood committed suicide eight months ago, and why young Dillon disappeared on the eve of his wedding and went to Africa. These are only two of innumerable cases I could mention.'

'Really this is preposterous, Mr. Crane,' broke in the fat man, his small eyes glittering with anger.

'The only thing preposterous about it,' snapped Lionel, 'is that so far you have been able to get away with it! But you won't for long, Kielmann. I'm not going to rest until I've put you in the dock, and your precious gang of crooks with you.'

He glanced contemptuously at Dawson and Morley.

'And I am thinking,' he added, 'that I've got to work quickly if I want to put you there before the White Friar gets you first.'

His last remark struck home. The faces of the three men before him blanched, and he saw the fear that suddenly sprang into their eyes at the mention of the menace that had already taken toll of two of their number.

'You thought you were being very clever, didn't you, Kielmann, when you shifted the blame of Rayland's murder on to the shoulders of your unknown enemy,' Lionel went on watching the stout man narrowly. 'But have you thought that you've got to reckon with him about it?'

Kielmann licked his dry lips.

'I see that the thought has only just

struck you. And he knows, Kielmann, for unless I'm very much mistaken it was he who sent me this wire this morning.'

He took the flimsy slip of paper from his pocket and unfolded it.

'Listen to this,' he went on. ''Ask Kielmann what he was doing at Horsham at eight o'clock this morning'.'

There was a dead silence as he put the telegram back in his pocket — a silence broken only by the rather laboured breathing of the stout man. At last with one of the greatest efforts he had ever made in his chequered career Mr. Kielmann pulled himself together.

'You do me an injustice, Mr. Crane,' he said his voice resonant with righteous indignation, 'But I bear you no malice. So many people have talked badly of me without cause. As for that telegram it is purely a libellous statement. I am not, I hope, a vindictive man, but I should very much like to meet the person who sent it to you — '

'Would you?' said a hollow voice. 'Well here I am — Death, who is never far away from you.'

They had their backs to the door, but at the sound of that toneless voice they swung round, three terror-stricken men paralysed to silence by fear. Only Lionel Crane remained his usual calm self, except that a light of intense interest gleamed in his eyes. There it stood just inside the doorway, the figure that Rayland had described. A long white robe enveloped the form, falling almost to the heels, and over the head was drawn a cowl-like hood that effectually concealed the face. One white-gloved hand gripped the doorknob, the other covered the occupants of the room with a long-barrelled ugly-looking automatic.

'I sent the telegram,' said the figure in white. 'I don't want to take credit for your work Kielmann. You shot Rayland — I saw you.'

'It's a lie!' whispered Kielmann hoarsely, his flabby face the colour of putty. 'A lie!'

'It's the truth and you know it,' went on the flat monotonous voice. 'Don't move Mr. Crane, I have no quarrel with you.' The muzzle of the automatic veered round a trifle in Lionel's direction as he started to take a pace forward. 'My only quarrel is with these — carrion.'

'Who — who are you?' stammered 'Slick' Morley and his voice was unrecognisable.

'I'm nobody — nothing,' said the figure by the door, 'An incarnation of living hate. To you and all your associates — death and destruction. Arnott's gone, Tison's gone. In good time you will all go — as Len Sutton went.'

'Len Sutton?' the husky croak came from the throat of 'Dude' Dawson.

'Yes, Len Sutton, who was done to death by Kielmann because he knew too much,' said the hooded figure. 'Len Sutton who was dragged from decency to a life of crime, and then shot like a mad dog. The police can't touch you, but I can, and you will suffer all the more because you will never know at what time the blow will fall, or who will be the next. It may be you, Dawson, or you, Morley. Or it may be Patricia York or Maurice. Only Kielmann knows that he will be the last.'

'Why are you carrying on this feud?'

asked Lionel Crane quietly. 'Why, if you know so much against these people, don't you place your information at the disposal of Scotland Yard, instead of resorting to murder?'

'Is it murder to wipe out vermin?' retorted the hollow voice. 'Would my bare word, unsupported by material evidence, suffice to bring these scoundrels to justice? You know that it would not. Even now the police have arrested an innocent man. It was I who shot Tison alone and unaided. Richard Venner should be released at once.'

Mr. Kielmann, staring with fear-laden eyes at the sinister form, found his voice.

'I don't know who you are,' he quavered, 'or why you should elect to persecute us like this, but if money is of any use to you, I'll give you fifty thousand pounds to leave us alone.'

A muffled chuckle came in answer behind the enveloping cowl.

'Give me the lives you have taken and the souls you have ruined,' said the hateful voice. 'Restore Len Sutton to what he was before he came into your clutches. No, Kielmann, you cannot bribe death, it's the one thing that all the gold in the world cannot alter, and — I am Death!'

The stout man shivered, and his face was wet with perspiration.

'Yet there is one thing you can give me,' the figure went on and its left hand was fumbling with the lock. 'You can give me the thing I have come here to take — the life of 'Slick' Morley in exchange for the life you took this morning!'

The long-barrelled pistol jerked up, there was a shattering report, and the tall figure of Morley sank limply to the floor — a tiny round hole in the centre of his forehead from which the blood oozed slowly.

The thing had happened so suddenly that Crane was taken completely by surprise, and before he could do more than take one step forward, the door had opened and closed on the wide-robed intruder and he was gone! Lionel's hand was on the knob when he heard the key click in the lock, and a moment later the slam of the front door. He tugged helplessly at the handle but the door had been locked on the outside, and then a heavy thud behind him caused him to turn round.

Mr. Alexander Kielmann lay crumpled in a heap on the carpet. For the first time in his life he had fainted!

8

Kielmann's Threat

Stepping over the body of the unconscious Kielmann and taking no notice of
the whimpering 'Dude' Dawson who was
crouched in a corner muttering and
mouthing to himself, Lionel Crane went
quickly to the window. It overlooked
Piccadilly and the Green Park, and
flinging open the lower sash, he leaned
out and was able to command a view of
the entrance to the block of flats. The
intruder in white could not yet have had
time, even supposing he had taken the
lift, to reach the ground floor. Crane was
hoping to catch a glimpse of him as he
left the building. He had noticed that the
white robe had been composed of almost
gossamer silk, and that it would be an
easy matter for the wearer to strip it off
and dispose of it under his coat.

A minute passed — two, but as yet no

one had come out of the entrance, and after watching for a further time, Crane turned to the cowering man in the corner.

'See if you can find something to break the door open with,' he ordered crisply. 'It's no use losing your nerve. There's a poker in the grate, use that. If you can smash a hole in the panel nearest the lock you ought to be able to get your hand through and turn the key.'

'Dude' Dawson nodded, and passing the body of Morley with a shiver, and averted eyes, picked up the heavy poker that Crane had indicated, and began to attack the door.

While he was so engaged Lionel turned his attention to 'Slick' Morley. The man was stone dead — one glance told him that. The bullet had struck him immediately above the bridge of the nose. He must have been dead almost before he reached the floor. Crane frowned and pursed his lips. Whoever the mysterious unknown was he was a magnificent shot, and evidently an expert in the handling of that difficult weapon — the automatic pistol.

A faint groan behind him made him

turn his head. The fat Mr. Kielmann was recovering and stirring faintly. Crane looked at him coldly but made no offer to help him in any way. One of the softest-hearted of men, he could find no atom of sympathy for that recumbent mountain of flesh, that concealed a heart as cruel and without pity as anyone he had ever known. Whatever Kielmann might be suffering and would suffer in the future, it could be but a tithe of the acute misery, and mental anguish that he had brought to his innumerable victims during his nefarious career.

As the stout man struggled dazedly to a sitting posture, the crashing blows on the door ceased, and Crane saw that Dawson had succeeded in breaking a way through large enough to admit his hand. A second later the key clicked, and the door was open.

'Get on the telephone to the nearest police station,' snapped Crane as the still trembling man flung the poker he had been using back into the grate. 'And ask them to come round at once. Tell them to send an ambulance and the Divisional-Surgeon.'

Dawson nodded, and staggered through the open doorway. He had scarcely disappeared from view before they heard his shrill scream of terror.

'What's the matter? What is it?' In two strides Crane was across the threshold and peering into the dimness of the hall.

'Come here quickly!' came the quavering voice of Dawson, hoarse with fear.

He was supporting himself against the wall with one hand, and gazing down at something that lay on the floor.

With a quick exclamation Lionel went over to his side. The something revealed itself as the manservant who had let him in.

He bent down. The man was still alive, and breathing heavily, and the faint sickly odour that was wafted to Crane's nostrils told him that he had been drugged.

'Where do the lights work from?' he asked and when Dawson mumbled an almost incoherent reply: 'Go and switch them on, will you.'

The other obeyed, and presently after much fumbling found the switch, and the centre pendant blazed into light. As it did so, Mr. Kielmann came unsteadily through the door.

'Don't tell me it's another death!' he whispered huskily as he caught sight of the figure on the floor. 'Good God, this is dreadful — terrible! I must have police protection. I insist that we have police protection.'

'If I had my way, you should have police protection for the rest of your life, Kielmann,' rapped Crane grimly. 'And that would be three clear Sundays before the execution.'

He straightened up.

'Go and telephone as I told you,' he went on addressing Dawson, 'and you' — he jerked his head at Kielmann — 'help me to carry this fellow into the sitting room.'

'Is he dead, too?' muttered the stout man approaching reluctantly.

'No, he's only drugged,' replied Crane shortly. 'Take his heels will you.'

Between them, Kielmann puffing and blowing like a grampus, they succeeded in carrying the unconscious man through the open door and laid him on the settee. He was already beginning to recover, and after Crane had bathed his head and administered some scalding hot coffee prepared by Dawson, he sat up dazedly and looked about him.

'My God, what — what was it?' he muttered shakily.

'You've been drugged,' said Lionel. 'If you feel strong enough I should like you to tell me exactly how it happened.'

The man nodded and moistened his dry lips.

'It was that fellow in white as did it,' he said. 'I was coming out of the kitchen when I saw the front door opening slowly, and I thought at first as how it was Mr. Kielmann who had been out for something. Then I saw it come in — all in white' — he shivered. 'I was as close to him as I am to you, but before I could scream or say anything he pressed something over my mouth, and I don't know nothing else until I woke up here.'

'Good Lord!' exclaimed Kielmann. 'The man, whoever he is, must have got a key to this flat.'

'He had a key all right,' said the

manservant. 'Oh, my head — it's awful!' He groaned and pressed his hands to his forehead.

'Lie down quietly for a few minutes,' replied Lionel, 'it'll go off. Did you get through to the police?' he asked turning to Dawson.

The pale but still immaculate gentleman nodded.

'Yes; they said they would send at once,' he answered, and crossing to the sideboard he poured himself out a neat whisky which he drank at a gulp. It brought a tinge of colour to his pale cheeks, though the glass rattled as he set it down.

'It's dreadful — simply appalling to think this man's got a key to the flat,' said Kielmann shakily. 'I shall have the lock changed today at once.'

'I don't think locks will save you, Kielmann,' said Crane grimly. 'The White Friar will get you at his own time,' and then abruptly, 'What's this story about Len Sutton?'

Mr. Kielmann started, but his expression was one of studied surprise, and

Lionel had to admit to himself that under the circumstances, the man's nerve was wonderful.

'Len Sutton?' The stout man spoke in a puzzled tone. 'I — know nothing about Len Sutton. I don't know whom he meant when he mentioned that name.'

'No, I didn't expect you would,' remarked Crane coolly. 'In fact, I was sure you wouldn't. It wouldn't pay you to know, would it, Kielmann. Listen to me,' a note of hardness crept into his voice. 'Len Sutton, whoever he was, is the reason behind the White Friar, Kielmann, and you know it — you've known it for some time. I'm going to make it my business to find out who Len Sutton was, and what happened to him. And when I've done that I don't think it'll be very difficult to put a name to the gentleman in white, who appears to have such a grudge against you and all your friends.'

He stopped and gazed steadily at Kielmann, but that large and fleshy man only licked his lips and remained silent.

'I'm going down to interview the porter,'

Lionel went on crossing to the door. 'Don't touch anything until I come back.'

He went out and they heard him close the front door gently. Dawson swung round on Kielmann.

'Did you hear what he said?' he exclaimed excitedly. 'He's going to start inquiring about Sutton, and if he does that — ' He broke off as Kielmann frowned and jerked his head towards the figure of the servant on the settee.

'Come into the other room,' he said, and, taking Dawson by the arm, led him into the hall.

'You fool!' he hissed furiously. 'Haven't you got any sense at all? Talking like that before Judd! He knows nothing about our business.'

'I'm sorry,' muttered the other. 'I forgot he was there.'

The stout man opened the door of the study and pushed Dawson inside.

'Now you can talk as much as you like,' he said shutting the door behind him. 'But whatever you've got to say, say it quickly. Crane will be back directly.'

'All I'm worried about is what he's

going to find out if he starts inquiring about Len Sutton,' said Dawson. 'Good Lord! There's no knowing what he'll discover if he does!' He took out a handkerchief and wiped his forehead nervously.

'He'll discover nothing,' snarled Kielmann. 'Pull yourself together and don't worry.'

'It's all very well to talk like that,' retorted his confrére sullenly, 'but Crane's not the police. He's like a bulldog when once he starts — he hangs on and never lets go. If he sets his mind to it he'll find out everything.'

Kielmann shook his large head and his teeth flashed in a mirthless grin.

'As I said before,' he answered, 'Crane will find out nothing.'

Something in his tone caused Dawson to look at him keenly, and the expression he saw in the stout man's eyes made him draw in his breath quickly.

'You're not thinking of — ' He stopped without completing the sentence.

'I'm thinking of — nothing,' said Mr. Kielmann and his voice was almost genial. 'But if Lionel Crane is so tremendously interested in Len Sutton that he wants to know all about it, I'll send him the same way as Sutton went. He'll know everything then — though his knowledge won't be much use to him!'

9

The Air-Gun

Lionel Crane went down to the ground floor in the automatic lift and made his way towards the uniformed porter, who occupied a little glass-partitioned office that faced the swing-doors that led to the street. The elderly man was reading the midday paper and looked up as Crane approached. In a few brief sentences Lionel made known his identity, and acquainted the horrified porter with what had happened.

'Has anyone been in recently?' he asked when he had finished his short recital.

The porter shook his grey head.

'No, sir,' he replied, 'Nobody's come in since you yourself, sir.'

'Or been out?'

'No, sir.'

'I didn't think they had,' murmured Crane with a tinge of satisfaction in his

127

voice. 'Now tell me have you got a list of all the people living in this building.'

'I haven't got a list, sir,' answered the porter, 'but I know them all. What name did you want?'

'I don't want any name,' said Lionel, 'but since the person who entered Mr. Kielmann's flat and shot his friend neither came in nor went out, it's not unreasonable to suppose that he lives on the premises.'

'Impossible, sir!' said the horrified porter. 'Everybody in this building is most respectable, sir. The landlord is very particular.'

Crane's mind flashed to the estimable Mr. Kielmann, and he smiled.

'However careful the landlord may be,' he said, 'he cannot hope to control his tenants' morals. Tell me who occupies the flats on the same floor as Mr. Kielmann.'

'Numbers twenty and twenty-one are occupied by Sir James Lavendale, and Mr. and Mrs. Combery,' replied the porter instantly. 'Sir James' flat, number twenty, is empty at the moment, as Sir James is abroad.'

'Oh, empty is it?' Lionel looked interested. 'I suppose you have a pass-key which fits all the front doors?'

The porter hesitated.

'Well, I have, sir,' he admitted, 'but I'm not supposed to — '

'Quite,' interrupted Crane. 'This, however is a special occasion. I should very much like to have a look at that empty flat, which is so conveniently near Mr. Alexander Kielmann's.'

'I don't know whether I ought to do it,' said the porter shaking his head dubiously. 'It's against all regulations, and without authority I don't think — '

'Here's your authority,' said Lionel crisply as a motor-ambulance drew up outside the door and three men got out. 'Here are the police.'

He greeted the tall man who entered with outstretched hand.

'How are you, Scott?'

Divisional-Inspector Scott gripped his hand with a smile of pleasure.

'Hello, Mr. Crane,' he said. 'It's a long time since we've met. How did you come to hear about this business?'

'I was there, when the man was killed,' answered Lionel, and quickly related what had occurred. 'I'm inclined to think,' he concluded, 'that the murderer is still on the premises. There is a flat on the same floor as Kielmann's that is empty at the moment, and I was arranging with the porter to have a look over it when you arrived.'

'I'll come with you,' said Scott and turned to the porter. 'Get your keys and take us up.'

The man went to a board at the back of his little office and took down a key.

'I hope you'll take full responsibility,' he grumbled. 'I'll get into trouble if — '

'That's all right,' broke in the inspector impatiently, 'I'll see that you're not blamed. Show us the way.'

The grey-haired porter shook his head, as though he disagreed entirely with the proceedings, and led the way towards the lift Crane and the inspector followed him, and Scott introduced the short, narrow-shouldered man who had entered with him as the Divisional Surgeon. The lift took them rapidly up to the floor on which the tragedy had happened, and Crane saw 'Dude' Dawson standing at the open door of Kielmann's flat.

'You'd better go in and have a look at the body, Doctor,' said Inspector Scott as they emerged from the cage. 'I'll join you in a few moments.'

The short man nodded without speaking. He was evidently sparing of words, for beyond a conventional remark when he had been introduced to Crane, he had uttered no other syllable.

'Take Dr. Freeman into the sitting room, Dawson,' ordered Lionel. 'You might have a look at the servant, Judd, too, doctor,' he added. 'He's had rather a nasty dose of chloroform.'

Freeman nodded again in reply, and passed into the hall with the immaculate Dawson. The porter was standing by a polished rosewood door that almost faced Kielmann's, and as they went over to him, he stooped and inserted his pass-key in the lock.

The flat belonging to the absent Sir James was almost an exact replica of Kielmann's, as Crane saw when they crossed the threshold and entered the square hall. It was well-furnished, and obviously the residence of a wealthy bachelor, for it lacked those subtle touches that give evidence of the presence of a woman's hand. They passed quickly from room to room, but the place was empty, and although Crane and the inspector peeped into every cupboard that was likely to provide a hiding place for a lurking intruder they found no one.

'It looks as though you were wrong, Mr. Crane,' remarked Scott as they came back to the sitting room.

Lionel nodded, his eyes absently scanning a row of silver-framed photographs that stood on the mantelpiece.

'It was only a possibility,' he answered, and then addressing the outraged porter who had followed them closely during their investigations as though afraid that they might take something. 'There are no other unoccupied flats in the building, I suppose?'

'No, sir,' was the reply.

'And you're still positive that no one went out after I came in?' persisted

Crane, his forehead wrinkled in thought.

'Positive, sir,' answered the porter. 'I've been in my box all the time, and saw nobody.'

'Well he must have got away somehow,' said Inspector Scott. 'Is there a back entrance?'

'No, sir,' the porter shook his head. 'There ain't no means of getting out, except by the front entrance.'

It was a puzzle. The man in white had apparently come from nowhere, shot 'Slick' Morley, and vanished into thin air. There was only one explanation, and that was that the murderer had a flat in the building, and simply walked from Kielmann's into his own. But the block was a large one, and contained over a hundred suites of apartments. With no clue regarding the unknown's identity, it was an impossible task to find him.

Lionel Crane pondered the matter in his mind, as, after leaving Inspector Scott in charge, he walked slowly back to his flat in Welbeck Street. He had a list of all the tenants of the flats, secured after a great deal of difficulty from the reticent porter, but it was practically useless at the present state of the case, although he intended to set enquiries going regarding them.

So far as he could see there was only one line of enquiry to make which was at all likely to lead to success. That was by trying to trace the mysterious Len Sutton, whom the unknown had mentioned. There was a distinct probability that if he could find out who Sutton was, and all about him, it would give him some clue to the man who had taken it upon himself to act as a Nemesis to Alexander Kielmann and his scoundrelly associates.

A big limousine car was drawn up opposite the kerb at his flat, and Crane looked at it as he inserted his key in the lock, wondering to whom it belonged. He was soon to find out, for Pollard greeted him as he mounted the stairs.

'There's a fellow waiting for you, Li,' said his partner. 'A Mr. Charles Mortimer. He says he's Richard Venner's uncle, and he wants to see you urgently.'

'Where is he?' asked Lionel. 'In the study?'

Pollard nodded, and Crane opened the door.

A white-haired old man with gold-rimmed spectacles and a pronounced stoop, rose as he entered and peered at him benevolently.

'Mr. Crane?' he asked in a curiously gentle and mellow voice.

'That is my name,' answered Lionel. 'I hope you haven't been waiting long, Mr. Mortimer.'

'It is immaterial how long I wait,' was the answer, and there was more than a hint of sadness in the tone. 'I have nothing else to do but to kill time. Once it was a different matter, but — ' he broke off. 'I have called to see you about my nephew, Mr. Crane.'

'So I understand,' said Lionel, seating himself in the chair opposite his visitor and looking at him questioningly, 'and I presume that it is in connection with his detention.'

Charles Mortimer inclined his white head.

'It's an absurd charge, sir,' he said. 'Dick is as innocent as you are. He's mentally incapable of committing such a crime.'

'I am happy to inform you, Mr. Mortimer,' said Crane, 'that there, is now no longer any question of his having committed it. The evidence was, I'll admit, sufficiently strong to warrant your nephew being detained on suspicion, but certain events which have taken place this morning completely exonerate him.'

The old man's lined face broke into a smile, and when Charles Mortimer smiled his rather sad, hard expression was transformed. His whole face became softened, and singularly kind.

'I am delighted to hear that,' he said. 'I had come here, Mr. Crane, with the intention of asking you to take up the case on my nephew's behalf. But it seems that I have, after all, had my visit for nothing. He will be released soon?'

'Immediately,' answered Lionel.

'Then I need no longer trespass on your valuable time,' said Mortimer. 'Perhaps if I called at Cannon Row I should be able to pick up my nephew and take him back with me to Horsham?'

'I've no doubt you would,' said Crane, rising as the old man picked up his hat and gloves, 'unless, of course, he has already gone.'

'I will take that risk, sir,' answered the other and held out his hand. 'I am very happy to have made your acquaintance, Mr. Crane.'

The detective shook hands with him, and was momentarily surprised at the strength of the old man's grip. Something of his surprise must have shown in his face, for Charles Mortimer seemed to read his thoughts.

'You were expecting rather a feeble grasp,' he said with a twinkle in his eye. 'I have been a great athlete in my time, Mr. Crane, and although now, alas, I am a semi-invalid, age and illness have not quite eradicated my early training.'

Lionel Crane conducted him to the door, and standing at the window watched the stooping, distinguished figure as it crossed the strip of pavement and got into the waiting car. There was something extraordinarily likeable about Mortimer, he thought, as he returned to his chair, and also something vaguely familiar. Somewhere he had seen that thin, aesthetic face surrounded by its crown of snow-white hair, before, but though he racked his brains he could not remember where.

He spent the afternoon writing long and detailed instructions to two agencies that occasionally worked for him, and the subject of these instructions was Len Sutton. He posted the two letters at tea-time, and returned to his study with the comfortable knowledge that he had wasted no time, and started his investigations along the line which, reason told him, was the only one that was likely to lead to the discovery of the unknown murderer.

Pollard had gone out to complete some enquiries concerning a minor investigation that they had on hand, and Crane, with a free evening before him, decided to clear up some outstanding work that had long been lying about.

He finished this at nine o'clock, and lighting his pipe, strolled over to the window with the intention of opening it, for the night was hot and oppressive; His hand was raised to the sash when without warning the glass splintered to fragments, as something buzzed angrily past his head. He ducked quickly, and the second bullet whizzed into the room and hit the wall with a smack. Cautiously he raised his head, until his eyes were above the sill. Quite a number of cars and taxis were passing in the street outside, and the shots could have come from any one of these. Lionel Crane smiled grimly, as he left the window. There had been no explosion, and he discovered the reason for this when he prised the bullet that had lodged in the opposite wall. It was an unusually large sized airgun slug.

Lionel had many enemies among the criminal fraternity of London, but he guessed the name of the man who had instigated that attempt on his life. And he guessed rightly, for ten minutes later the Frenchman, Maurice, who had fired from the interior of a saloon car was apologising to an angry and disgruntled Mr. Kielmann for his failure.

10

The Listener at the Door

Nearly three weeks passed without any sign or appearance of the mysterious avenger whose mission in life seemed to be the extinction of the Kielmann gang, and Mr. Kielmann began to grow a trifle less uneasy and also less watchful.

Since the shooting of 'Slick' Morley, he had had a fresh and stronger lock put on his front door, and as extra precaution had persuaded 'Dude' Dawson to vacate his own comfortable flat, and take up his abode in the spare bedroom. Dawson, as a matter of fact, had required very little persuading, but had jumped at the invitation with alacrity. Although for the time being their fear of the unknown was quiescent, it had by no means vanished. There were times in the middle of the night when Kielmann would start awake from a troubled sleep, and lie shivering and bathed in perspiration at some sound, which turned out to be nothing more alarming than the slamming of a door by a late resident of the flats, or the backfiring of a car in the street below. But for the past weeks a disturbing factor had come to bother the smooth Mr. Kielmann's peace of mind, and this was no less than Lionel Crane's untiring activity in trying to trace Len Sutton.

Twice since the episode of the air-gun had the stout man tried to remove this new menace to his safety, and on each occasion the result had been failure. The poison he had caused to be put in Crane's early morning milk which was always left outside on the steps, proved to have had no effect, for Lionel was apparently in the habit of testing this before it was brought to the table, and the car which had tried to run him down in Oxford Street, had only succeeded in smashing into a lamppost, and the driver had been fined twenty pounds by an unsympathetic magistrate, which sum had eventually come from Mr. Kielmann's pocket.

The worst of it was that although he had no real evidence, Crane knew from whom these various attempts on his life emanated, and Mr. Kielmann guessed that he knew. What he did not guess was how much Lionel had succeeded in finding out about Len Sutton, and this worried him more than a little. The strain of it all had taken effect even on Mr. Kielmann's iron constitution.

He was thinner, and the sudden wasting of his flesh had resulted in giving him somewhat the appearance of a half-inflated balloon, for the skin hung loosely below his eyes and about the corners of his mouth, and covered his collar in wrinkled folds. There was not a movement that Crane made at that time that was not instantly reported to him. He was aware that the two agencies were working diligently, and that Lionel himself was giving them a personal hand in the inquiries that were being instituted, but try as he might he could not find out the result. He had on one unforgettable day even gone so far as to call on Crane himself, giving as an excuse the reason that he was anxious to learn if anything had been discovered concerning the man in white who had shot down 'Slick' Morley, and for half an hour Lionel talked home truths to him, letting him know plainly that he was perfectly aware of the real reason for his visit, Mr. Kielmann had eventually left the flat in Welbeck Street a little more uneasy than when he had entered it, without having garnered any of the information he had gone to so much trouble to obtain. It was getting near ten o'clock on the evening of a day approaching the end of the third week since the killing of Morley when Mr. Kielmann sat in his comfortable study talking to 'Dude' Dawson, and Patricia York. He sat in the study because the sitting room had become rather distasteful to him since the tragic event that had happened there, and these days he kept it locked.

'Something's got to be done about that interfering fellow,' he said pouring himself out a generous helping of whisky and squirting in a minute quantity of soda. 'I'm more afraid of him than I am of the other chap.'

'You've tried three times to do something about him,' remarked Dawson with the hint of a sneer, 'and nothing's happened.'

Mr. Kielmann's eyes glinted dangerously.

'You can stop using that tone just as quick as you like,' he snapped. 'It wasn't my fault that those attempts were failures. It was the bungling way in which they were carried out.'

Patricia York stretched out a slim white arm, and helped herself to a cigarette.

'You've got to get up very early in the morning to catch Crane,' she said looking across at the stout man with a pair of childish blue eyes. 'He's a smart guy.'

Kielmann nodded, watching her as she lit the cigarette and puffed daintily.

'He may be a smart guy, as you call it,' he replied, 'and really, Pat, I wish you'd cut out that American stuff. It jars on me.'

She shrugged her shoulders, and he went on;

'The trouble is, I've been too careful.'

'Dude' Dawson raised his eyebrows in surprise.

'What do you mean — too careful?' he asked.

Mr. Kielmann drank long and slowly, and with evident enjoyment before replying.

'All the plans I have suggested for putting Crane out of the way have been too simple,' he said putting down his glass. 'They have left too much to chance. Now I've got a new idea, and I think that this time we shall be successful.'

'Well, let's hear it,' grunted Dawson.

'You know that warehouse we've got along the river near Lambeth,' said Mr. Kielmann, carefully testing the end of a cigar, and 'Dude' Dawson went pale.

'The place where Len Sutton was — ' he began.

'Exactly,' the stout man interrupted him. 'The place where Len Sutton passed to a better world — or let us hope so.'

He paused, applied a match to the cigar, and puffed until it was alight to his satisfaction.

'Well what about it?' asked Patricia York impatiently, picking up her cigarette from the floor where it had dropped from her fingers at the mention of the name. 'What's that got to do with Crane?'

'Only that I'm thinking of taking him there,' replied Mr. Kielmann easily.

Dawson rapped out an oath and leaned forward with a jerk.

'Are you mad?' he cried angrily, 'or is this your idea of a joke.'

'Neither,' was the cool reply. 'If you'll only keep quiet and listen, I'll explain.'

Dawson shrugged his shoulders and leaned back in his chair.

'Go on,' he said shortly.

'That's better,' nodded Mr. Kielmann approvingly. 'Now we've tried to get Crane at his flat, and in the street, and we've failed. The last attempt cost me twenty pounds, too,' he added sadly. 'It's useless trying anything more on those lines. The only thing we can do is to get him somewhere where he can't get away, hence my reference to the warehouse.'

'It sounds all right,' grunted 'Dude' Dawson. 'But how do you propose to get him there? Ask him to tea?'

The stout man blew a cloud of smoke ceilingwards and watched it disperse.

146

'Not quite so simple as that,' he said, 'but very nearly. There is an empty house to be sold at the far end of Lolworth Grove, Putney,' he suddenly went off at a tangent. 'It's rather a charming property, and I'm going to the agent tomorrow — or rather you are — to obtain the keys.'

'Thinking of buying it?' inquired Dawson sarcastically. 'Look here, I don't know whether all this trouble has turned your brain, but — '

'My brain was never better, 'Dude',' declared Kielmann. 'If you had half my brain you'd still have half more than you've got. I told you just now to keep quiet and listen, didn't I? Well, then, do so.'

'You must admit that you're rather talking in riddles,' said Patricia crushing out the stub of her cigarette in the ashtray.

'Well, if I am, I'll give you the answer to them,' retorted Mr. Kielmann with a flash of teeth. 'Listen carefully. As I said there is an empty house at Putney, of which you will obtain the keys tomorrow as a prospective buyer. Once you've done that, we will send a little note to Crane purporting to come from the gentleman who uses the picture of a White Friar as a visiting card, asking Crane to meet him at the empty house, and stating that he will then reveal his identity, and tell a story that will surprise him. There will be only one condition, that Crane is to come — alone. If he attempts to bring anybody with him, the appointment will not be kept.'

'And you think he'll do that,' sneered Dawson. 'Why he'll have the place surrounded by police.'

'Oh no, he won't,' said Kielmann shaking his head. 'I know Crane better than you do. He'll play a lone hand. We'll make the appointment for twelve o'clock, midnight. Once he enters the grounds of that house we've got him.' He slowly clenched a white hand as he finished speaking.

'And when you've got him, what are you going to do with him?' asked Patricia languidly.

'We shall have a car waiting and take him to the warehouse, and then' — the stout man paused and showed all his teeth in an expansive smile — 'and then he can go and find Len Sutton,' he ended softly.

'Why go to all this bother over the house?' said Dawson. 'Why not make an appointment direct at the warehouse?'

'Oh, yes,' said Mr. Kielmann caustically, 'an excellent idea! And if anything goes wrong there is irrefutable proof that the warehouse belongs to me, and is used as a store place by the Amalgamated Textile Company. No, if by any chance Crane should be shadowed or bring anyone with him, there is nothing to connect us with the empty house at Putney and — What's that?' he whispered, suddenly breaking off in the middle of his sentence.

'What's what?' asked Patricia, her eyes widening with fear.

'I thought I heard a sound — as if there were someone outside in the hall,' said Kielmann in a low voice.

'Judd, probably,' said Dawson.

'Judd's out,' the stout man rose and went softly over to the door. 'Keep quiet a minute.'

He gripped the handle noiselessly, and a pistol had appeared as if by magic in his hand. With a sudden wrench he flung the door wide and darted out into the hall. They heard the sound of a faint scream, and then Kielmann came back dragging somebody by the arm behind him.

'Who — ' began Dawson, and stared in blank amazement as the stout man flung his captive into a chair.

'Mary Rayland!' said Kielmann gazing at the terrified and shrinking girl. 'Perhaps you will kindly tell me what the dickens you were doing in my flat, listening at the door?'

11

A Shock for Dawson

Mary rubbed her arm where Mr. Kielmann's strong fingers had bruised the soft flesh, but she remained silent.

'Lost your tongue, have you?' asked the stout man pleasantly. 'Well perhaps in some respects, it's just as well. I don't like people who talk too much, particularly when they discuss my business. What were you doing in my flat, and how did you get in?'

She stared into the large, flabby face, thrust so close to her own, and her eyes reflected the fear that filled her soul, but she uttered no word, merely compressing her lips a little tighter.

'So you're not going to answer, eh young lady?' There was the hint of a menace behind the gentle purring voice. 'Well, I hate being rough with women — particularly beautiful women — but — '

He shot out a hand and gripped her wrist. 'If you don't tell me what you were doing listening outside my door, I'll make you wish you'd never been born!'

The cold, matter of fact way in which he spoke, made the girl shrink back with an involuntary cry. It was far more terrifying than any outbreak of temper could have been. There was something inflexible, utterly callous and cruel in that flat, even voice that seemed to shrivel up the last shred of her courage.

'I wanted — I wanted to find out something about you,' she stammered almost inaudibly at last.

'Oh, I see,' Kielmann laughed mirthlessly. 'You wanted to find out something about me, did you? And what was this something that you wanted to find out?'

It was a long time before the girl replied, and when she did her voice was steadier.

'I wanted to find out what you had to do with my father's death,' she said.

For a moment Mr. Kielmann staggered, but quickly recovered himself.

'Dear me,' he said sarcastically, 'was

that it? Is that why you went to the trouble of entering my house like a burglar? Well, well, you might have saved yourself a lot of bother. I had nothing to do with your father's death. He was killed by the same person who shot my friend, Tison.'

'I don't believe that,' answered Mary. 'Neither does Mr. Crane.'

'Oh, you've been talking it over with him, have you?' remarked the stout man, 'Does Crane accuse me of the crime?'

She shook her head.

'No,' she replied, 'but he thinks you had some hold on father, and were trying to blackmail him, and were afraid that he might give you away.'

'I see,' Kielmann spoke in a low, pleasant, almost conversational voice. To anyone who knew him it betrayed the fact that he was in a most dangerous mood. 'Did Crane send you here?'

Again Mary shook her head.

'No, I came on my own account,' she answered.

'Thinking you would try a little detective work for yourself,' sneered the stout man. 'Charming! Perfectly charming! How did you get in?'

The girl made no reply, but her eyes strayed for a second to her handbag, which had fallen on the floor beside her. The acute Kielmann noticed the momentary glance.

Stooping suddenly, he picked up the little bag, and opened it. Putting in a chubby hand he extracted a peculiar-shaped, flat-toothed instrument, and his mouth expanded into a wide smile.

'How very professional!' he remarked holding it up. 'One of the latest picklocks! Really, my dear young lady, you show a remarkable ability for burglary. You ought to adopt the business.' And then suddenly changing his bantering tone: 'How long had you been listening outside the door?'

'Not very long,' answered the girl, but her eyes dropped before the cold gaze.

'H'm! Not very long is rather vague,' said Kielmann.

He frowned thoughtfully, twisting the pick-lock between his finger and thumb, and for some time there followed a strained silence. Then all at once the wrinkles between his eyes smoothed themselves away like magic, and his teeth gleamed.

'Get on the phone to the garage, Dawson,' he ordered sharply. 'And ask them to send the car round in five minutes.'

'Dude' Dawson, a silent, and it must be confessed a rather troubled audience, opened his mouth to speak.

'What — ' he began, but Mr. Kielmann snapped him up.

'Don't talk,' he said harshly. 'Do as I tell you.'

The immaculate Dawson looked at him curiously, and then with a slight shrug of his shoulders, went over to the phone, and gave a number.

Mary glanced uneasily at the stout man, and rose to her feet.

'I think I'll go now,' she said in a rather embarrassed tone, for the situation was decidedly uncomfortable.

She was annoyed with herself at having been caught in circumstances that were hardly creditable to herself, though she had heard enough from the other side of the door to warrant the reckless impulse which had sent her to spy on Kielmann.

'Not for a few minutes, if you don't mind,' remarked the stout man smoothly. 'Pray don't deprive us of your company so soon.'

'But I want to go,' she insisted moving towards the door. 'I'm sorry I — '

She broke off as Kielmann interposed his vast bulk between her and the door.

'You shall go almost directly,' he said. 'In fact, I have ordered my car for you. It's unpleasant for unattended young ladies to walk about the West End of London at night, and I should never forgive myself if anything happened to you.'

Something in his eyes terrified her, and her heart went cold.

'I would much prefer not to wait for the car, thank you.' She exercised all her willpower to prevent her voice shaking, but was unsuccessful. 'It's very kind of you — '

She stopped with her heart beating wildly, as he advanced towards her, and caught her by the arm.

'You will wait for the car, all the same,' he said, and then dropping his pretence of friendliness, 'You little fool! Do you think I'm going to let you get away after what you must have heard?'

'I heard nothing,' she stammered. 'Nothing!'

'You may not have heard anything,' grated Kielmann. 'On the other hand, you may have heard a great deal. In either case I'm not taking any risks. You will wait here until the car arrives.'

'Dude' Dawson hung up the receiver and turned round.

'They're sending it along at once,' he reported.

'Good,' said Mr. Kielmann. 'Go down and wait for it, and tell the man who brings it round that I shan't require him, I shall be driving myself.'

'What's the game?' asked Dawson, and the stout man glared at him.

'Will you do as you're told without asking fool questions?' he roared, and Dawson went out hastily.

'I'll not wait,' cried Mary in a sudden

panic. 'What are you going to do with me?'

'You'll know very soon,' retorted Kielmann, and as she opened her mouth to scream, he clapped a fat hand over it. 'I shouldn't advise you to try that,' he hissed. 'If you will put your head into the lion's mouth, you must expect him to bite you.'

She struggled desperately but the stout man was capable of unexpected strength, and held her easily. Still keeping one hand over her mouth so that she could make no sound, Mr. Kielmann looked across at Patricia York who was watching the proceedings with an air of studied indifference.

'Go to the left-hand top drawer of my desk, Pat,' he ordered, 'You'll find a silver case and a small blue bottle. Get them quick!'

Patricia nodded and going over searched in the drawer. With fear in her heart Mary watched her take out a flat case and a bottle. Guessing what the contents were, she redoubled her efforts to break away from the iron grip that held her, but it was useless. Although she did not know it, Mr. Kielmann had been an expert in the science of ju-jutsu in his youth, and still retained his knowledge.

'There's a syringe in that case,' said the stout man, 'Open it, and screw it together.'

Patricia obeyed, coolly and collectedly without a trace of excitement, or even interest in her baby face. For all the world she might have been cleaning a cigarette-holder so little emotion did she display.

'What next?' she enquired as she finished screwing the delicate needle to the end of the barrel.

'Fill it from the bottle, and give it to me,' said Kielmann.

Mary saw her deliberately insert the needle in the narrow neck of the blue bottle and pull back the plunger, and in her last supreme panic she opened her mouth and sank her teeth viciously into the podgy hand that pressed her lips. With a snarl of pain Mr. Kielmann jerked his bleeding hand away, and at the same instant Mary tore herself from his grasp. She gave one scream and leaped for the door, but even as her trembling fingers touched the handle, the stout man recovered himself. With surprising agility for his size he bounded over to her and dragged her back into the middle of the room.

'Quick, give me the syringe!' he panted, flinging her roughly into a chair, and stretching out an arm towards Patricia.

Mary screamed again, but he choked the sound in her throat, and the next moment she felt a sharp pain in her arm. Almost immediately her whole body began to grow numb and lifeless, and the room swam before her eyes. She tried desperately by sheer will power to ward off the blackness, which seemed to rise up and envelop her. But it conquered, descending with a suddenness that was like the extinguishing of an electric light, and she slipped into oblivion.

Mr. Kielmann looked down at her, nodded in a satisfied way, and going over to his desk laid the hypodermic syringe that he had used with such good results, on the blotting pad.

'The little spitfire!' he muttered examining his lacerated hand. 'Good job I happened to have that drug near by.'

'What are you going to do with her?' enquired Patricia York, in a level voice, lighting a cigarette.

'Have her taken to the warehouse at Lambeth,' replied Mr. Kielmann. 'Here, bind this up for me, will you.'

He took a clean handkerchief from his pocket, and held out his hand.

'Isn't it rather risky?' said Patricia as she tore the linen into strips and began to deftly bandage the wound. 'It's nine chances to one the porter saw her arrive here.'

'I've thought of that,' answered the stout man with a smile. 'You and she are almost the same height and build. In a few moments you will put on the hat and coat she is wearing, and go home, taking care to keep your face concealed. If there should be any inquiries the porter will then be prepared to swear that she left this building, and that lets us out.'

'You're clever, aren't you, Kielmann?' said Patricia admiringly as she skilfully knotted the ends of the bandage.

'I have always had the reputation for using my brains,' admitted the stout man modestly.

'How are you going to get the girl out?' asked the woman resuming her cigarette.

'These flats,' said Kielmann, 'are inhabited by several bachelors, who although by no means rowdy, are not always strictly — er — teetotal. Before you make the change in costume I have suggested, you will array the young lady in a suit of Dawson's evening clothes — there's a spare one in his bedroom. The fit would not, I'm sure, be Saville Row, but a light overcoat and the bad light in the vestibule, of which I have repeatedly complained, will cover a multitude of — er — discrepancies.'

Patricia stared at him for a minute, and then her own red lips parted in a smile, and she laughed softly.

'I see,' she said nodding her shingled head. 'She will enact the part of one who has dined not wisely but too well.'

'Exactly,' Mr. Kielmann displayed his teeth, 'Supported by her intimate friends,

'Dude' Dawson and myself, she will be conveyed with much hilarity to the waiting car. No doubt the porter will be scandalised, but I have a very good reputation here. So being used to the behaviour of the young men I mentioned before, he will merely come to the conclusion that I have been entertaining one with a like fondness for strong waters.' He chuckled, and was still chuckling when 'Dude' Dawson entered.

'The car's here,' he announced, 'and I've sent the man back to the garage,' and then catching sight of the smiles on the faces of Patricia and Kielmann, he added; 'What's the joke?'

'An excellent one, my dear Dawson,' said the stout man good-humouredly. 'An excellent one,' and proceeded to acquaint the immaculate man with the details of his plan.

'You'll have to be quick,' grunted Dawson looking rather dubious. 'We can't leave the car outside unattended for long.'

'We're not going to.' Kielmann went over to the unconscious girl, and stooping picked her up in his arms.

'I'll carry her into the next room, and Patricia can do the necessary change.'

'Dude' Dawson nodded, and held open the door. Kielmann went out with his burden, followed by Patricia and after a moment or two came back, and joined the other. Dawson was pouring himself out a drink and glanced inquiringly at the stout man as he squirted in a minute quantity of soda.

'Just a small spot,' said Mr. Kielmann, and as the other was again about to use the syphon, 'No soda — I'll have it neat.'

He gulped down the drink and smacked his thick lips.

'Who's going to take the girl to the warehouse?' asked Dawson helping himself to a cigarette.

'You are,' replied Mr. Kielmann carefully, and the immaculate crook grunted.

'I don't like it,' he said without enthusiasm. 'I — '

'Whether you like it or not, you'll do it,' the stout man's voice was hard. 'That girl must be got rid of, Dawson. She must have been listening long enough to have heard what we were saying with regard to

Crane. If she gets away and goes to him'
— he made an expressive gesture — 'we
shall all find ourselves cooling our heels
in a cell in twenty-four hours.'

'What have I got to do with her when I
get her to the place?' grumbled Dawson.
'I'll have nothing to do with any killing. I
draw the line at that.'

'Have I asked you to do any killing?'
snarled Kielmann. 'All you'll do is to tie
her up and gag her and leave her in the
room which Len Sutton used. I'll be
along at four o'clock to attend to the rest.'

'Dude' Dawson looked at him and
shivered, but he made no comment,
and then waited in silence for the return
of Patricia York. She came back at the
expiration of about ten minutes, wearing
Mary's hat and coat, and Mr. Kielmann
eyed her approvingly.

'You'll do,' he said shortly. 'If you keep
your head down, and well buried in that
fur collar, nobody would suspect that
you weren't the Rayland woman. Did you
dress her in Dawson's suit?'

Patricia nodded.

'Yes,' she answered, 'it's a fairly good

165

fit. At any rate good enough to pass.'

'Then we'd better get off,' said Kielmann. 'Make sure the porter sees you go out, and take a taxi. Tell the driver to take you to the railway station for Horsham, and then take another from there to your own flat. I'll phone you tomorrow.'

'Anything else?' asked the woman, and he shook his head.

'No that's all,' he said. 'Now go.'

She went without another word, and Kielmann turned to Dawson.

'We'll wait for another quarter of an hour, and then we can stage our little comedy,' he remarked.

'How long is the girl likely to remain under the dope?' said Dawson.

'At least two hours,' was the reply. 'Ample time to get her to the warehouse.'

There was another long silence while they watched the minutes slowly creep away. At last Kielmann rose to his feet, and laid down the cigar he had been smoking.

'Put your coat on,' he said briefly.

Dawson passed out into the hall,

slipping into a heavy overcoat, which he took from the stand. Twisting a muffler round his throat, he followed the stout man into his bedroom. Mary lay on the bed, and Patricia had done her work well, for it was the slim form of a young man in evening dress that they gazed down upon.

'The only thing that gives her away is her hair,' muttered Kielmann. 'We shall have to hide that under a hat.'

He went back into the hall, and returned with a soft felt hat and a light coat.

'This will do,' he said. 'Help me to put this coat on her.'

They succeeded in getting the coat on the limp form, and when Kielmann had crushed the hat over Mary's short wavy hair, he surveyed his handiwork with satisfaction.

'Not so bad,' he remarked approvingly. 'Now for the supreme test. You take one of her arms, and I'll take the other.'

They raised the light figure of the unconscious girl from the bed and propped her upright between them. Kielmann, being the shorter, placed one of her arms round his neck, and Dawson put his arm through the other.

'Now, come on,' said Kielmann, 'we've got to get this over before Judd comes back.'

They met nobody going down the main staircase, but even if they had it is doubtful whether they would have given the two men supporting a drunken third between them, more than a second's glance. As they reached the vestibule Mr. Kielmann began to talk in a loud and remonstrative voice.

'Really this is most unpleasant,' he said for the benefit of anyone who might be about, and for the porter in particular. 'I'd no idea Harvey would allow himself to get in this disgusting state. It really is preposterous. I've no sympathy for men who cannot leave drink alone, or haven't the strength of mind to know when they've had enough.' Out of the corner of his eye, he saw the porter peering at them from his little glass cubicle.

'I sincerely hope, Dawson, that you will have a talk with him tomorrow, and try and cure him of this distressing habit. It is appalling for so young a man to get like this.'

'I'm afraid he won't take any notice of me,' said Dawson. 'He's always rather partial to whisky, but I've never known him as bad as this before. Pull yourself together, Harvey old man,' he addressed the sagging form between them.

'You ought to have warned me,' said Mr. Kielmann irritably. 'I would have seen that he stopped before it was too late. Nothing annoys me so much as drunkenness.'

They had run the gauntlet of the lighted vestibule and the porter, and reached the street. The car was waiting by the kerb, and beside it was the uniformed figure of a policeman. Dawson felt his heart sink. Were they going to be detected after all?

'You can't keep this car here any longer,' said the officer of the law as they staggered across the pavement, and then seeing the state of the third member of the party, 'Hello, what's the matter? Is the gentleman ill?'

'It's all right, constable,' said Kielmann.

'My friend has — er — unfortunately drunk more than was good for him. We are taking him home.'

The policeman grinned.

'Oh, I see,' he said. 'Well, so long as you get that car away at once, it will be all right. My word, 'e must 'ave 'ad a good time!'

He watched while they bundled the 'inebriated gentleman' into the back of the saloon, and then with Mr. Kielmann's substantial tip jingling in his pocket, strolled away.

Kielmann watched 'Dude' Dawson climb into the driving seat and move away, and then as the car disappeared in the direction of Piccadilly Circus, re-entered the vestibule with a contented smile on his lips.

It was just striking eleven when Dawson pulled up outside a high wooden gate in a narrow street in Lambeth that ran parallel with the river, and getting out of the car searched in his pocket for the key. Admittance to the warehouse owned by the Amalgamated Textile Company was gained through a courtyard that gave on to a disused wharf, and after unlocking the heavy padlock that secured the outer gate, Dawson propped it open and made his way among the piles of rubbish and broken packing cases to the door that led into the warehouse itself.

He gave an involuntary shiver as he inserted the key in the lock and pushed the door open. There arose before his eyes the vision of a thin, unshaven, pale young man whose home this had been, and whom he had last seen sitting at a rickety table, sketching idly in that very place. With an effort he put the unpleasant picture from his mind, pressed down the switch of the electric light which bathed the narrow passageway in a dim yellow glow from the dusty bulb, and leaving the door open picked his way across the yard to the waiting car.

He glanced sharply up the dingy street before he opened the door at the back, but there was nobody about, and twisting the polished handle he pulled the door open and leaned into the dark interior.

The next moment he started back with a choking cry that was almost a sob.

Something cold and hard was pressed against his forehead, and a hollow, mocking voice said:

'I've been waiting for you, Dawson. Know any prayers? If you do, you'd better say them quickly, for tonight you are face to face with death!'

'Dude' Dawson caught sight of a white cowled head in the filtering rays of a nearby streetlamp, and knew that his end was at hand!

12

The Diamond Bracelet

THE LAMBETH MYSTERY!
Dead man found in Wharf Street!
What is the meaning of the White Friar?

Shortly before twelve o'clock last night Police-Constable Elliot made a startling discovery in Wharf Street, a narrow thoroughfare near the river in Lambeth. While patrolling his beat he came upon the dead body of a well-dressed man in evening clothes lying in the gutter beside an empty saloon car. The man had been shot dead, the bullet having struck him in the forehead. The absence of any weapon proves conclusively that it is a case of murder.

The peculiar feature is the fact that lying on the body when the constable discovered the crime, was an ordinary visiting card — such as can be obtained at any stationers — on which had been drawn in ink the picture of a Friar in a white robe.

From papers found in his possession the murdered man's identity has been established as that of Mr. Montague Dawson, a director of the Amalgamated Textile Company, outside the entrance to whose warehouse he was found.

A curious fatality seems to hang over the members of this firm, for it will be remembered that Mr. James Arnott, Major Tison, and Mr. Everard Morley have all within the past few weeks met their deaths under violent and mysterious circumstances. And in each case the card with the figure of the White Friar has figured prominently.

What is the hidden meaning attached to this token?

The police are very reticent, but we understand from Scotland Yard that they are working on a clue, and further developments are expected shortly.'

Mr. Alexander Kielmann dropped the morning newspaper on the floor beside

174

his chair, and his face was old and grey. So his unknown enemy had got 'Dude' Dawson. That only left Patricia York and the Frenchman, Maurice, before it was his turn. Well, he wasn't going to wait for that. There was a chance to get away, and he was going to take it.

Leaving his untasted breakfast he went into his study. Sitting himself at his desk, he unlocked a drawer, and took out his bankbook, and the sight of the respectable balance lying to his credit did something towards restoring his shattered nerves.

In fluid money he had something over a hundred thousand pounds, and by selling up certain securities that he held, during the next few days, he could raise almost an equal amount. With that nest-egg, he would start afresh in some far-off country where the laws of extradition did not operate, and where there would be no menacing figure in white waiting to pounce on him at an unexpected moment. There had been no mention of the girl in the newspapers, he suddenly remembered with a frown. What had happened to her? Dawson had certainly not taken her into the warehouse before he met his death, for he — Kielmann — had gone there as he had arranged, and had almost run into the police who had taken charge of the place. So where had she gone? The only explanation was that the killer of Dawson had taken her away with him.

Kielmann felt that if he could be sure of this, he would be greatly relieved, for he had been hourly expecting a visit from the police demanding an explanation concerning Mary Rayland, and his treatment of her. So far nothing more formidable than a host of reporters had disturbed him, and these he had resolutely refused to see.

He was engaged in checking up his various holdings from a little notebook when Patricia York almost burst into the room.

'I've just heard,' she gasped, her voice shaking and the pallor of her face showing even through the thick makeup she had daubed hastily on her cheeks. 'About Dawson. It's awful — ghastly! I'm going to get away today. I can't stand it any longer! I'm going to quit.'

Mr. Kielmann made no reply, he went on writing until he had finished what he was doing, carefully blotted the sheet, and looked up.

'So you're going to quit, are you?' he said wearily. 'Well, I think it's the best thing you can do — if you can do it.'

The girl looked at him quickly. 'What do you mean — if I can do it?' she asked,

'Exactly what I say,' answered the stout man. 'You've overlooked an important fact.'

'What's that?' demanded Patricia suspiciously.

'You've overlooked the White Friar,' said Mr. Kielmann, and enjoyed the look of terror and consternation that came over the girl's face. 'For all we know he may have planned to get you next.'

She sank into a chair as her knees gave way beneath her, and with a shaking hand, took a cigarette case from her bag.

'Who do you think it is?' she quavered making several unsuccessful attempts to light a cigarette.

Mr. Kielmann shook his large head.

'I don't know,' he answered. 'If I did know' — his voice hardened — 'all danger in that direction would be at an end. I'd treat him the same way as Len Sutton was treated.'

He paused and looked at her sharply, an idea suddenly crossing his mind.

'You first got hold of Sutton,' he went on. 'At Monte Carlo, wasn't it?'

She nodded and shivered.

'Yes, but why rake that up? I don't — '

'Because I want to know something,' cut in Mr. Kielmann abruptly. 'Did he ever tell you anything about himself?'

'No. I tried to make him, but he never would talk about his past. The only thing I knew was, that he was of good family and had been to Oxford.'

The stout man rubbed his many chins gently, and his eyes narrowed.

'I've got a theory that it's someone connected with Len Sutton — a relation probably,' he said speaking almost to himself, 'who is trying to wipe us out. Of course, Sutton wasn't his real name.'

'What does it matter what his real

name was,' said Pat impatiently. 'All that matters is that we've got to clear out before it's too late. I want my share of the money.'

'All right, you can have it — this afternoon,' answered Mr. Kielmann. 'Come back here at four o'clock. There'll be more to come to us now that the others are — er — out of the way which is something to be thankful for.'

The girl rose to her feet and flung away her cigarette.

'You're a cold-blooded beast, Kielmann,' she said without emotion. 'I believe you'd murder your own mother if it was likely to put money in your pocket. You've got no heart at all.'

'A heart,' said Mr. Kielmann with a flash of white teeth, 'is an expensive commodity if used in any other way but as a pumping-machine. Come back at four o'clock and your money will be waiting for you.'

* * *

Lionel Crane also read the newspaper account of the death of 'Dude' Dawson, and within a quarter of an hour of having done so, was walking up the stone staircase that led to Detective-Inspector Herrick's office at Scotland Yard.

'Hello, Mr. Crane,' greeted the inspector looking up from a report on his desk as Lionel entered. 'Glad to see you. I suppose you've heard the latest?'

'If you mean about 'Dude' Dawson, yes,' said Lionel with a smile. 'That's why I've come to see you.'

Herrick pushed aside the document he had been reading and leaned back in his chair.

'It's a staggerer, Mr. Crane,' he grunted. 'Whoever this fellow is, he must have got a pretty strong motive for hating the Kielmann crowd. By Jove, there's only three left now out of that bunch — Patricia York, André Maurice and Kielmann himself.'

Crane nodded gravely.

'Yes, he's been pretty thorough,' he said. 'I wonder who's going to be the next?'

'God knows!' said Herrick. 'There's not the ghost of a clue in the Dawson business, except the used cartridge shell which we found in the saloon.'

'In the saloon?' Crane raised his eyebrows. 'Then the murderer must have shot him from the interior of the car.'

'Yes; curious isn't it?' remarked the Scotland Yard man.

'Very,' Lionel knitted his brows. 'It was Kielmann's car, I suppose? There's no doubt about that?'

'Not the slightest. We got on to the garage. Dawson ordered it last night to come round to Kielmann's flat.'

'Strange. Dawson would hardly have been driving the man who killed him,' said Crane. 'Stranger still is his reason for being at Lambeth at that hour of the night. Have you seen Kielmann about it?'

'No, I was going round when you came in,' answered Herrick. 'Perhaps you'd like to come with me?'

'I should,' said Lionel, 'and I should like to have a look at that warehouse. I suppose you couldn't get a search warrant?'

Herrick shook his head dubiously.

'I'm afraid not,' he replied. 'We've got

no reason to apply for one. Why, what do you expect to find there?'

'Nothing definite,' said Crane candidly. 'But I should like to have a look round all the same. You haven't discovered anything about Len Sutton, have you?'

The burly inspector shook his head again.

'No, nothing,' he answered, shrugging his square shoulders. 'I've tried every source I know, and nobody appears to have heard of Len Sutton. For all I can find out about him he might never have existed at all.'

'My agents are in the same boat,' said Crane, 'They can't pick up the slightest trace. Yet I am convinced that Sutton did exist, and in some way he's at the bottom of this mysterious individual who calls himself the White Friar.'

'Perhaps he's Sutton,' suggested Herrick.

Crane pursed his lips.

'Possible, but I don't think so,' he said doubtfully. 'My opinion is that Sutton was somebody whom Kielmann did to death. I'm almost certain he's not alive

— either he committed suicide, or Kielmann killed him. That's how I look at the meaning of the words the man in white used before he shot 'Slick' Morley.'

'In either case,' objected Herrick, 'we should have heard about it. A man can't kill himself, or be killed by somebody else without his body being discovered.'

'No, but Len Sutton might not have been the name by which he was known,' said Crane. 'It might only be the name by which the Unknown knew him. Suppose, for instance, he had no friends or relations, in that case providing there was no proof of his identity — '

He broke off as Herrick brought his big fist down on the table in front of him.

'By jove! Mr. Crane!' he exclaimed excitedly. 'Do you remember the feller who was pulled out of the river some weeks ago? He'd been shot through the head, but we couldn't find out who he was or anything about him. Nobody was reported missing, and the whole thing was a mystery. We concluded he had been killed by a gang of river thieves, but we've never been able to substantiate that theory. Suppose he was Len Sutton?'

'I remember the affair,' said Lionel, and his eyes gleamed. 'He was found just by Blackfriars Bridge. I shouldn't be surprised if you're right, Herrick, but it doesn't help us much. If I remember rightly you published photographs of him at the time.'

'Yes, we took them at the mortuary, and had them circulated to every newspaper in the country,' grunted the inspector, 'asking anyone who recognised him to come forward but nobody came.'

'So you see, if no one knew him at the time,' said Lionel, 'it's not surprising if we can't find anybody who does now.' He paused and stared at the window thoughtfully. 'I wonder — ' he added and stopped.

'What?' asked Herrick slowly rising from his chair and lifting down his hat and coat from a peg behind the door.

'He was found in the river,' murmured Crane, 'and Kielmann's warehouse is on the river bank. If that unknown man was Len Sutton, Herrick, there might be a connection.'

'There probably is,' growled the Scotland Yard man struggling into his coat. 'But you can't prove it. That's the trouble with Kielmann — he's so deuced clever you can't prove anything.'

'Kielmann will get his deserts, Herrick,' said Crane as he followed the inspector along the corridor. 'But I don't think it will be at the hands of the law.'

They took a taxi to Piccadilly, and discovered that Mr. Alexander Kielmann was out.

'We'll come in and wait,' said Crane when he heard from Judd, who opened the door to them, that he was expecting his master back at any moment.

The servant reluctantly showed them into the study.

When he had withdrawn and left them alone, Crane looked round.

'I'd like an hour alone in this flat,' he said, 'though I doubt very much if Kielmann is fool enough to keep any evidence about.'

'He isn't,' said Herrick. 'Some months ago when we began to suspect him of being on the crook, we managed to get a

search warrant — and we found absolutely nothing.'

'It's only about once in a hundred years
that one comes across a really clever crook,'
said Lionel his eyes roving about the comfortable room. 'As a rule they are a fairly
brainless lot, and easily caught — ' He left
the sentence unfinished, staring at an armchair by the fireplace.

'What's the matter?' enquired Herrick
quickly following the direction of his eyes.

For answer Lionel crossed over and
picked out from between the leather
cushion of the seat and the upholstery
something that sparkled in the light from
the window.

'What is it?' asked the Scotland Yard
man eagerly as he held it up.

'A diamond bracelet,' said Crane softly,
'and the last time I saw it, it was on the
wrist of Mary Rayland.'

'Mary Rayland?' gasped Herrick in
astonishment. 'Then how the devil did it
get here?'

'That,' answered Crane, 'is a question I
shall have much pleasure in asking Mr.
Alexander Kielmann!'

13

The Missing Girl

He had scarcely finished speaking when they heard a key grate in the lock of the front door, and the next moment Kielmann himself entered briskly. He seemed to have entirely recovered from his shock of the morning, for his smile was radiant and he carried himself almost jauntily.

'Making yourselves at home, gentlemen?' he greeted raising his eyebrows in momentary astonishment at seeing them. 'That's right. I suppose you've called to see me about poor Dawson. Terrible affair, Mr. Crane, terrible! I read of it in the newspapers this morning, and have been expecting a visit from the police ever since. I don't know the object of these attacks upon my colleagues, or who is at the bottom of it, but if the intention is to frighten me, they haven't attained their object. I — '

He broke off, his eyes staring and his jaw dropped, glaring at the glittering thing in hand. If nothing else had succeeded in frightening him, as he boasted, this certainly had, to judge by the expression that came to his flabby face. It was only transitory however, for with a supreme effort he recovered himself.

'That's rather a pretty ornament you have there, Mr. Crane,' he said boldly, coming over to Lionel's side. 'Where did you get it?'

'I found it almost hidden under the cushion in your armchair, Mr. Kielmann,' answered Crane coolly.

'My armchair?' repeated the stout man in well-simulated amazement, though he was inwardly cursing himself for not having noticed and moved such a damning piece of evidence. 'How on earth did it get there? It looks like a lady's bracelet.'

'It is a lady's bracelet,' retorted Lionel, 'and it happens to belong to Miss Rayland.'

The ready-made explanation for the presence of the piece of jewellery that had flashed to his mind, Kielmann discarded instantly, and his brain worked quickly. There was scarcely a second's pause before he softly laughed, and replied cheerfully:

'Well that accounts for it then. Miss Rayland came in to see me for a few minutes last night.'

Crane felt a reluctant admiration for the quickness with which the man had handled what must have been a thoroughly unpleasant situation for him.

'I didn't know she knew you,' he said.

'She doesn't — or rather she didn't,' answered Mr. Kielmann instantly. 'She came to return the — the transfer of shares which poor Tison had taken to her father on the evening he was killed.'

It was a possible explanation and but for that momentary hesitation, Crane would have been almost inclined to accept it.

'I'm surprised she should have taken all the trouble to come all the way from Horsham for that,' he said eyeing the other steadily. 'She could so easily have posted it.'

'There's no accounting for what women will do,' answered the stout man returning his gaze without the blink of an eyelid. 'Probably she had to come up to town for something else, and thought she would kill two birds with one stone. Is there any particular point in these questions Mr. Crane? Has anything happened to Miss Rayland?'

It was a daring question to ask under the circumstances, for so far as Mr. Kielmann knew Mary Rayland might have already communicated with the police, and related her adventures of the previous night.

'Not that I'm aware,' replied Lionel and the stout man breathed an inward sigh of relief. 'I was merely curious to know how this came to be in your flat.'

'She sat in that chair,' said Kielmann, 'I suppose the thing slipped from her wrist without her noticing it.'

'That is most likely what happened,' agreed Crane. 'The clasp is broken. I'll take it and send it back to her.' He dropped the piece of jewellery into his pocket, and Mr. Kielmann experienced a twinge of uneasiness. If Crane got into communication with the girl, she would probably tell him all that had transpired at the flat, and it was just the chance that the police had been waiting for. Up to now there had been nothing tangible to warrant them interfering with Mr. Kielmann's liberty, but Mary Rayland, if she liked, could bring a definite charge against him, and a serious charge at that, for the attempted abduction of young and beautiful girls is looked upon by the powers that be with an unsympathetic eye.

However, there was nothing for it. He would have to take the risk, and after all, that night would be the end of it. A big wad of notes in his breast-pocket represented his entire liquid assets which he had just drawn from the bank, and if the worst came to the worst, he'd have to be content with that not inconsiderable sum, and leave his shares until such time as he could with safely sell them out through the medium of a broker in some distant land. So with a bland smile which it must be confessed was somewhat

191

forced and a wave of his podgy hand he dismissed the bracelet, and looking at Herrick said in his accustomed soft, purring voice:

'I presume that it was something else that you called to see me about, gentlemen?'

The Scotland Yard man nodded shortly. He did not like Mr. Kielmann, and made no attempt to disguise the fact.

'I came to see you about this murder,' he said gruffly. 'From what we can gather the shot that killed Dawson was fired from the interior of your car. Can you offer any explanation to account for that?'

Mr. Kielmann shook his head, and spread out his hands with a dissenting gesture.

'Why on earth should I be able to suggest any explanation?' he protested. 'I'm not a detective. That is, surely, a job for the police?'

'Yes, that is why I'm here,' grunted Herrick. 'I understand from your garage, that you ordered your car to be sent down here last night, and the man who brought it was told he was not wanted, as you would be driving yourself. Is that correct?'

'Quite correct,' replied the stout man.

'Did you use the car?' went on the inspector, and Mr. Kielmann shook his head again.

'No, I ordered it for my friend Dawson,' he answered.

'Where was he going — to the warehouse?' asked Herrick.

The stout man hesitated for the fraction of a second before he replied.

'No. What he was doing in the vicinity of the warehouse is as much a mystery to me as to you. I ordered the car for him to take home a friend of his who had — er — dined with me, and who had unfortunately partaken of too much liquid refreshment.'

'You mean he was drunk?' said Herrick bluntly.

'A vulgar word, but expressive of his condition,' agreed Mr. Kielmann sorrowfully. 'Yes, he was undoubtedly drunk.'

He congratulated himself inwardly on this explanation, for if they inquired of the porter which they were almost certain to do, the man would substantiate his story.

'What was your friend's name?' asked Crane.

Mr. Kielmann coughed, and continued to cough for some time. For the life of him he couldn't remember the name he had invented on the spur of the moment for Mary on the preceding evening. He remembered calling her something, but what it had been he couldn't for the life of him think.

'Excuse me,' he spluttered choking realistically. 'A slight — er — irritation of the throat. I am — er — subject to these attacks.'

'Usually when you are asked a rather awkward question,' said Lionel sarcastically. 'Don't hurry yourself, Kielmann, we've plenty of time.'

The stout man recovered, and mopped his forehead.

'What was it you asked me?' he inquired a little breathlessly.

'I asked you the name of your inebriated friend,' said Lionel.

'Oh, yes.' There was nothing for it, thought Kielmann rapidly. He would have to invent a name and trust to luck that

194

the porter would not remember either. 'Er — Roberts — Cyril Roberts.'

'Where does he live?' Crane went on.

At this request Mr. Kielmann was completely nonplussed. He might invent a name but it was impossible to invent an address to fit it.

'I really don't know,' he answered innocently. 'You see he was poor Dawson's friend, not mine.'

'I see,' said Crane feeling more than suspicious that the whole story was a lie. 'I suppose he doesn't live at your warehouse by any chance?'

'Certainly not,' said the stout man, 'nobody lives there.'

'Not even Len Sutton,' snapped Lionel suddenly, and Kielmann almost reeled.

'What do you mean?' he asked huskily his face the colour of putty.

'Nothing,' answered Crane, and then grimly: 'Kielmann, there was a man pulled out of the river at Blackfriars Bridge a few weeks ago — shot through the head, and with nothing to identify him. Was that Len Sutton?'

It needed more than an effort to regain

his composure, but Kielmann managed it though his forehead glistened with the strain.

'Really, Mr. Crane,' he said evenly. 'I don't know whom you mean when you talk about Len Sutton. I think I told you that before: I have never known anyone of that name in my life. Do you believe that?'

'No,' answered Lionel truthfully. 'I do not!'

He and Herrick took their leave shortly afterwards, having failed to elicit any information, whatever, and stopped in the vestibule to question the porter.

'Oh, yes,' he remembered Mr. Kielmann's drunken friend all right.

'Properly soused, he was,' said the man with relish. 'I've seen some drunks in my time, used to be on the door at Black's Club in the days when a gentleman's club was a gentleman's club. But nothin' to beat the feller you're talkin' about, sir. He was so tight he couldn't even move 'is legs.'

'Then how the devil did he manage to walk?' demanded Herrick irritably. An interview with Mr. Kielmann always upset his never very smooth temper.

The porter grinned.

' 'E didn't,' he retorted. ' 'E 'ad to be 'eld up like a sack of coals between Mr. Kielmann and Mr. Dawson. And all the time Mr. Kielmann was sayin' 'Pull yeself together, 'Arvey, it's disgraceful' — '

'Harvey?' interrupted Crane, sharply. 'Are you sure he said Harvey?'

The man looked surprised.

'Yes, sir, positive,' he answered. 'Why what — '

'It's all right,' broke in Lionel and looked at Herrick significantly. 'It seems curious that Kielmann called him Harvey, and told us his name was Roberts,' he whispered to the Scotland Yard man.

Herrick scratched his chin.

'It seems as though he was trying to conceal his identity,' he muttered perplexedly. 'But why?'

Crane's brows drew together in a frown, and for a second or two he stared thoughtfully out of the door at the stream of people passing in Piccadilly.

'What time did this gentleman call on

Mr. Kielmann?' he asked abruptly.

'It's funny you should ask that, sir,' answered the porter shaking his head. 'Do you know I've been puzzling about that ever since last night.'

'Why?' Lionel's eyes suddenly gleamed with a swift light of sudden interest.

'Well, sir, because I never saw 'im come in at all,' said the man. 'I suppose he must have slipped by me while I wasn't looking, but it's curious, because the gentleman in flat 4, left me a note to give a friend he was expecting, and I was watchin' for 'im most of the evenin'.'

'H'm! He must have come early,' commented Lionel. 'Did you see a young lady come in?'

'I saw two, sir,' replied the porter. 'Which do you mean — Miss York or the other lady?'

'The other lady,' said Crane.

The porter nodded.

'Yes, sir, she asked me the number of Mr. Kielmann's flat. I saw her come in, and I saw her go out.'

'Oh, you saw her go out, did you? Are you sure of that?' Crane felt a twinge of disappointment. A vague idea that had occurred to him was shattered by the porter's statement.

For the moment he had wondered if anything had happened to Mary Rayland in Kielmann's flat.

'Yes, sir,' answered the man emphatically. '1 saw her go — I'm certain of that.'

'Was she alone, or was the other lady, Miss York, with her?' enquired Lionel.

'She was alone,' declared the porter. 'She left just before Mr. Kielmann's friend.' He paused and rubbed the back of his head. 'That's funny, too, sir,' he went on, 'because I never saw Miss York leave at all.'

'You never saw Miss York leave?' repeated Crane quickly. 'Were you in your box all the evening?'

'Yes, sir — till I closed the outer door at twelve.'

It was with a very thoughtful expression on his face that Crane walked down Piccadilly by the side of the Scotland Yard man, and for some time he uttered no word. Then suddenly he looked at his companion.

'Herrick,' he said, 'there's a mystery here. Patricia York visits Kielmann and never goes out. An apparently drunken young man whose identity Kielmann seems most vague about, goes out, but according to the porter never went in. What do you make of that?'

'Nothin',' grunted the inspector, 'unless you're trying to suggest that the drunken man was Patricia York.'

'I'm not,' answered Lionel shortly. 'There's no reason why Patricia York should masquerade as a drunken man. No, I'm suggesting that the drunken man was Mary Rayland.'

The Scotland Yard man stared at him in astonishment.

'But the porter saw her go out,' he protested.

'Or thought he did,' corrected Lionel quickly. 'But supposing the person he thought was Mary Rayland, was Patricia York dressed in her clothes, then the mysterious goings and comings of these people would be explainable.'

'Good Heavens!' gasped Herrick. 'You don't mean — '

'I mean,' answered Crane, 'that it's my belief that for some reason or other Kielmann wanted to kidnap Mary Rayland. He drugged her, dressed her in a man's clothes and got her into the car — '

'But what was he going to do with her?' broke in the Scotland Yard man.

'Take her to the warehouse at Lambeth,' replied Crane crisply, 'and that's why Dawson was there when he met his death.'

'Then if you're right,' demanded Herrick, 'where is Mary Rayland now?'

'If she isn't at home,' said Lionel, 'I don't know, unless — '

'Unless, what?' grunted the inspector.

'Unless, she's been carried off by the man who shot Dawson,' said Crane.

They were passing a post office in Shaftesbury Avenue as he made his last remark, and with a word of apology to Herrick, Crane left him and went inside. It was nearly a quarter of an hour before he came back, and his face was grave.

'I've just been on the telephone to Horsham,' he announced. 'Mary Rayland left her house yesterday afternoon, and hasn't been home since!'

14

The Share Out

At four o'clock that afternoon in accordance with their previous arrangement, Patricia York called on Mr. Alexander Kielmann to collect the share due to her from her long association with that gentleman. She found him beaming benignly from behind his desk at the Frenchman, Maurice, who had been summoned by telephone to attend the share out, and the reason for Mr. Kielmann's large and expansive smile was an unexpected piece of luck which had come his way during the course of the early afternoon.

His broker had rung through to inform him that he had been able to unload the bulk of Mr. Kielmann's shares on to another client, and with joy in his heart, the stout man had arranged for the money to be sent to him by special messenger in cash.

There was nothing now to prevent him carrying out his plan, and making his getaway early on the following morning, and the addition to the already large wad of money which he carried in his breast-pocket, would be most comforting.

Kielmann had been a busy man for the past few hours. Many months ago he had foreseen the possibility of having to make a hasty exit from the country, if not exactly of his birth, for that was a trifle indefinite, at least the hunting ground of his more successful enterprises, and with this in his mind he had kept his passport up to date. The aeroplane that was to take him across the Channel had already been chartered, and was due to leave Croydon at six o'clock on the following morning. In fact, everything that could be done, had been done, and in consequence Mr. Kielmann was feeling in a particularly benevolent mood, and at peace with the world.

'Come in, Patricia, come in,' he greeted taking the cigar from his lips as the woman entered. 'Everything is ready for you.' He waved his hand towards two packages of money that lay in front of him.

'How much have I got?' she asked eyeing the parcel of notes greedily.

'Just on sixty thousand pounds,' said the stout man genially, 'and for most of it you have to thank our friend the Unknown. Otherwise if there had been more to split up amongst, it would have been considerably less.'

He pushed one of the packages towards her, and picking it up she ran the edges of the notes through her fingers and dropped it into her bag and it was characteristic of her that now she had finished with Kielmann and got her money she did not even trouble to go through the formality of thanking him.

'When are you leaving, and where are you going?' he asked curiously.

'I'm leaving tonight,' she answered. 'Where I'm going — well, that doesn't matter to you does it?'

He ignored the hard, almost insulting tone from the woman who had once been only too willing to do his slightest bidding, and shook his head.

'No, perhaps after all it's better if you keep your information to yourself,' he said. 'The less you speak of it, the less chance it will have of reaching the ears of — the White Friar.'

He watched with secret amusement the colour fade from her cheeks.

'He'd have to be very clever if he could catch me,' she said defiantly, though her lips trembled. 'By this time tomorrow I shall be out of his reach for good.'

It was the truest thing she had ever said, but she did not know it then.

'Well, I've got a lot to do,' she went on turning towards the door, 'and not much time to do it in. So I'll be going. So long!'

'Goodbye, Pat,' said Mr. Kielmann, 'and good luck!'

'The same to you,' she answered, and nodding to the silent Frenchman she went out.

Patricia York had a flat in a block of buildings about halfway up Oxford Street, and since there were several things that she wanted to buy, she elected to walk. Going through the park would bring her out at Marble Arch, and as this was near the shops she wished to visit, she strolled leisurely along Piccadilly towards Hyde Park Corner.

As she turned into the Park, a man coming hurriedly in the other direction bumped into her heavily, knocking her bag from under her arm. The encounter was so violent that it threw her off her balance, and before she could recover herself she stumbled and fell.

The cause of the collision was full of apologies, and with many remarks concerning his clumsiness, to which Patricia replied rather snappily, helped her to her feet and retrieved her bag. She glanced into it to see if the money was still there, and finding that it was, cut short the other's protestations and inquiries as to her personal welfare, and went her way. The incident passed out of her mind almost at once, but later she was to remember it as full of significance.

She spent the rest of the afternoon shopping, and returned to her flat shortly before six to be greeted by her maid with the information that a gentleman had called to see her.

'A gentleman?' said Patricia frowning. 'Who was it?'

She numbered a good many gentlemen among her acquaintances but none were on calling terms.

'I don't know, madam,' answered the girl, 'but he was most anxious to see you. He waited for some time, and then said he couldn't wait any longer, but would call back again later.'

'Did he give any name?' asked Patricia.

The maid shook her head.

'No, madam,' she said. 'He wouldn't. He said you wouldn't know him.'

'You'd no right to let a strange man come in,' said her mistress sharply. 'What was he like?'

About this the maid was decidedly vague, and beyond the fact that he had been elderly and very well-dressed could give little information.

Patricia ordered some tea, and while she sipped the steaming beverage pondered over the identity of the visitor.

She could think of no one whom it could be. At first the idea that it was a detective flashed to her mind, but she dismissed this almost at once. She had always been careful in all her dealings, and there was nothing the police could get hold of to pull on her. Possibly it was a tradesman to whom she owed money.

There were several of these, for Patricia lived extravagantly, and ordered without thought of the bills that would inevitably follow. Well, she had the means of settling them anyway.

She took the package of money from her bag, and looked at it complacently. It was intact as Kielmann had given it to her, for she had paid for her recent purchases with some notes that she already had in her possession.

Finishing her tea she set about her packing, and it was late in the evening before she strapped and locked the last of her numerous trunks and hatboxes. She had already sent her maid away — the girl was a daily and did not live in the flat — and now feeling hungry she rang the service bell, and to the waiter who answered the summons gave an order for a light meal. There was a restaurant attached to the flats in which she lived, and this had partly been the inducement for Patricia having taken one, for she loathed work of any kind, particularly cooking.

She had an hour and a half before the car she had ordered to take her to Southampton was due to arrive, and lighting a cigarette, she wandered round the tiny flat to see if she had overlooked anything. There was nothing left that she wanted to take, and she had visited the agents that morning, and paid her rent up to date, so all she had to do now was to leave the key in an envelope, and walk out. Her meal arrived and she ate it leisurely, her mind filled with rosy prospects of the future. It had always been a wish of hers to visit America, and this was her intention. Her passport was in order, and the lights of Broadway called her.

She sat for some time sketching out her plans for the future, and was eventually aroused from her reverie by the return of the waiter for the tray. She had spent all her other money, and had to pay the man with a note from the wad Kielmann had given her. He departed to get change, and presently returned with a curious expression on his face.

'I'm sorry, Madam,' he said rather curtly, 'but I can't change this.'

'Why?' she asked in genuine surprise.

'The cashier says that it's a wrong 'un.'

'A wrong un?' Unconsciously she echoed his phrase.

'A bad one, a forgery,' he said.

He held it out, and she took it from him. It was a clumsy forgery — even she could see that now that she was really looking at it — and laying it down on the table she went to her bag and took out another.

'I'm terribly sorry. It was quite a mistake,' she said, and was giving the second note to the waiting man when she saw that that was a forgery, too.

With a sudden feeling of panic, she pulled out the thick bundle and examined them one by one. They were all bad, and executed in the clumsiest fashion.

A wave of anger swept over the woman. Kielmann had done this! He had tried to double-cross her!

With an exclamation of rage she dashed the bundle on to the floor. All her plans had fallen in ruins. It was useless the car coming now, because she had no money. She had spent all she had on the things she had bought that afternoon. Going into her bedroom she crushed on her hat, and slipped her arms into the sleeves of her coat. She would go round and tackle Kielmann at once, making him give her good money instead of that useless muck. Hurrying back to the sitting room she found herself, confronted by the waiter who in her rage and disappointment, she had for the moment forgotten.

'What about my bill?' he asked truculently.

She had begun a hesitating explanation when there came a loud and imperative knocking on the front door. Breaking off in the midst of a sentence, and wondering who it could be, Patricia pushed past the waiter, and going out into the little lobby, opened the door. Two men stood on the threshold, and pushing past her they entered without ceremony.

'What do you want?' she asked angrily. 'How dare you — '

'Is your name Patricia York?' asked the taller of the two, and when she nodded: 'I'm Detective-Inspector Sorrel of Scotland Yard, and I've got a warrant for your arrest.'

'My arrest?' she gasped. 'Nonsense! There must be some mistake. With what am I charged?'

'Being in possession and uttering forged Bank of England notes,' said the inspector gravely, and Patricia swayed and caught the edge of the door for support.

'That's right,' interjected the waiter who had followed her out into the hall. 'She tried to do it on me. Crikey, ain't she a beauty!'

'There must be some mistake,' cried Pat wildly. 'I know nothing about forged notes, I tell you, nothing!'

'They never do when they're pinched,' said the Scotland Yard man with a grin. 'The ignorance of the criminal classes is shocking. But we've had information to the contrary.' He turned to the man who was with him. 'Go and search that bed,' he ordered. 'According to information received you should find a whole heap of slush under the mattress.'

He caught hold of Patricia's arm as the other went away to carry out his instructions, and led her into the sitting room.

'You might as well take it quietly,' he advised.

'But I'm innocent!' she screamed loudly.

'It's a 'frame-up', they all say that,' replied the stolid detective. 'It's a stock phrase. Hello!' he stooped and picked up the scattered notes on the floor, looking at them and whistled. 'Phoney, every one of them. I guess you're innocent all right.'

Before she could reply, the other man came back from the bedroom carrying a thick packet in his hand.

'You were quite right, sir,' he said, 'I found these under the mattress. They're all forgeries.'

The inspector took them and nodded.

'I think we've got you, young lady,' he said. 'You'll get seven years for this, or I'm a Dutchman,' then, as he was putting the bundle in his pocket, 'Hello, been going in for drawing? How did this get here?'

Patricia York saw the visiting card, and the sketch of the robed man on it and understood.

That night she slept in a comfortless cell in Cannon Row police station instead of the luxurious cabin she had booked on board the *Atalania*, and her sleep was troubled by visions of a white-cowled menacing figure that flitted like the shadow of death through her uneasy dreams.

15

Kielmann's Warehouse

The information that had resulted in the arrest of Patricia York had reached Scotland Yard by special messenger shortly after six o'clock. It had been in the nature of a typewritten letter without signature or address, and merely stated that if the police paid a visit to the girl's flat that evening, they would find definite and convincing proof regarding her guilt as a passer of forged money, and discover a considerable quantity of bad notes under the mattress of the bed in her bedroom.

The Yard are in the habit of receiving countless communications of this kind, most of which turn out to be false. But it is their duty to act upon 'information received,' and in this case they were all the more eager because Patricia had been for a long time marked down as a suspected person, though the uttering of false notes was not among the various enterprises of which she was suspected.

Inspector Sorrel reported her arrest, and the result of his visit to her flat to Detective-Inspector Herrick, and within twenty minutes that energetic official was ringing Lionel Crane's bell, at Welbeck Street. He found Lionel engaged in pacing up and down his study, and he greeted the Scotland Yard man with a smile, and waved his hand towards a syphon and glasses and box of cigars.

'Help yourself to a drink and a smoke,' he said knocking out the ashes of his pipe into the fireplace, and immediately proceeding to refill it from the jar on the desk. 'What's the latest news? I can see you're simply bursting with something.'

Herrick flung his hat on the settee, and poured himself out a generous helping of whisky.

'The York woman was arrested this evening,' he grunted gulping down the neat spirit, and smacking his lips with satisfaction. 'Sorrel found her flat full of 'slush'.'

He proceeded to give a brief and concise account of what had happened. Crane listened with drawn brows.

'Of course, it was a 'frame-up',' he commented when Herrick finished. 'Patricia is the last person in the world to risk passing bad money.'

The Scotland Yard man nodded, and bit off the end of one of Lionel's Coronas.

'I agree with you,' he answered, 'and equally, of course, our unknown friend who has sworn to exterminate the Kielmann gang is at the bottom of it. But Patricia will find it a dickens of a job to prove, and I can see her going down for a seven stretch.'

'She deserves it,' said Crane. 'I've no sympathy for her. Although she may not be guilty of this, she is guilty of worse crimes. Crimes that are utterly impossible to bring home to her. She has acted as the decoy for Kielmann and his friends for years, and is directly responsible for the dozens of unfortunate victims that have found themselves in his net. She is only meeting with justice at last, and by now is probably experiencing a little of the despair that she has brought to the hearts of others more innocent than herself.'

'Sorrel says that she was obviously on the point of making a getaway,' said the inspector. 'She had packed everything, and while he was there a car arrived from a hire company to take her to Southampton. The *Atalania* leaves for New York in the morning, so it's not difficult to guess her destination.'

'Then all I can say is that the White Friar has proved a benefactor to the American nation!' answered Crane. 'There's only Kielmann and Maurice left now.'

'Yes and I'll bet neither of them are feeling too comfortable,' grunted Herrick. 'Of course they don't know yet what's happened to Patricia; and when they see it in the newspapers tomorrow, they'll guess who's responsible, and the knowledge will make that fat scoundrel squirm, I'll warrant.'

'I very much doubt whether Kielmann will see it in tomorrow's papers,' murmured Crane softly.

The inspector set down the glass containing his second drink, untasted, and shot a quick glance at him.

'What do you mean?' he snapped. 'You don't think that anything will happen to him — '

'No,' broke in Lionel quickly, 'nothing like that. But Kielmann has chartered a special airplane for six o'clock tomorrow morning, and before the papers are published I should say he would be well away.'

'How do you know that?' said Herrick.

'I've been expecting him to try and make a getaway for days,' answered Crane, 'and I concluded that he would try to leave by air, so I planted an agent at all the aerodromes with instructions to notify me if anyone answering to Kielmann's description tried to book a plane.'

The Scotland Yard man frowned.

'I see,' he said. 'So he's going to clear out while the going's good, eh? Well, we can't stop him, unfortunately. There's not a scrap of evidence against him.'

'I know,' Lionel shrugged his shoulders irritably. 'At the same time I should like to know the exact moment that he leaves. I've come to the conclusion that the only way to find out the identity of Kielmann's mysterious enemy is to watch Kielmann. Sooner or later they will meet, and I think the time's coming soon.'

'You're probably right,' assented Herrick. 'Have you got somebody watching Kielmann then?'

Crane nodded.

'Yes, Pollard,' he replied. 'He's been trailing him all the afternoon. By the way, did you make any further enquiries about Mary Rayland?'

'I set the usual routine working,' answered Herrick. 'Notified all stations, and circulated a description of her.'

'I'm rather worried about that girl,' muttered Crane. 'Where the deuce can she be? She certainly never returned home, so either she's in Kielmann's clutches, or else in the hands of the man who shot 'Dude' Dawson.'

'Why should either of them want to detain her?' grunted the inspector.

'Because in all probability she knows too much,' retorted Lionel. 'Self-preservation is a very strong motive. She must have been a witness to the death of Dawson.

If we are right she was in the back of Kielmann's car, as Dawson drove away from Piccadilly.'

Herrick drained his glass, and banged it down on the table.

'Well I shall be glad when the whole case is over and done with,' he snorted. 'It's too vague for my liking. There's nothing to get hold of, no clue that one can work on. We know Kielmann's a crook, but we can't arrest him without evidence. We know that some mysterious person killed Arnott, Tison, Morley and Dawson, and had Patricia York locked up, but we don't know who. We've heard a lot of talk about a man called Len Sutton, who never seems to have existed, and whom we can't trace, and now to cap it all, Mary Rayland has disappeared into thin air. We haven't the faintest idea why, or who's responsible. I've never been in charge of a case that was so unsatisfactory or so lacking in clues.'

'No, it is rather a tangle,' admitted Crane. 'However, it will probably straighten itself out if we're patient.'

'Patient?' Herrick rose to his feet, and

reached for his hat, jamming it tightly on his head. 'You've got to combine the patience of Job with the mentality of a fortune-teller to get any further with this business. Well, so long, Mr. Crane. I'm going home.'

He shook hands with Lionel and took his departure. Crane heard the slam of the front door, and with a little smile playing about the corners of his mouth dropped into an easy chair before the fire.

For some time he sat staring at the grate, turning over in his mind a plan that had occupied his thoughts all day. In spite of the lack of evidence against Kielmann there must be something somewhere that would prove the methods by which that smooth and elusive man had amassed his fortune — documents that would be conclusive. It was impossible that he could have carried on his gigantic blackmailing business without accumulating a mass of papers that could not be destroyed. The question was, where were these kept?

Certainly not at Kielmann's flat, for twice on one pretext or another that had been raided by the police without the slightest result. There was a possibility that Kielmann rented a safe either at his bank or at a deposit, but since, for the purpose of his nefarious business, it would be necessary to have access to these letters, etc., Crane thought it rather unlikely.

There remained the warehouse at Wharf Street, and this seemed to him to be far the most probable place. It would have been easy for Kielmann to have arranged some secret hiding place in the building accessible at all hours of the day or night, where he could keep the essential tools for his unknown trade — the indiscreet letters that enabled him to screw money from his unfortunate victims, evidence of past, and in many cases, long-forgotten crimes, which this ruthless man collected and used to terrorise the chief people concerned, to his own pecuniary advantage, possibly some reference that would clear up the mystery of Len Sutton, and the unknown menace that hovered over Kielmann like the Angel of Death.

The more Crane thought it over, the more convinced he became that the warehouse by the river was the place where the evidence necessary to put Kielmann in the dock was to be found, and he decided on a bold plan. He would visit the place that night himself, and search for the hiding place he more than suspected to be concealed there. It was illegal, of course, and if he were caught would require a lot of explaining away. But it was, so far as Crane could see, the only chance ot getting Kielmann, and he had taken too many risks during his life to worry much about the consequences.

It was getting near to half-past eleven when he rose to his feet, and began to make preparations for putting his plan into execution. Going into his bedroom he changed quickly into a thick suit of tweed, and from a drawer in the big wardrobe took out a fat leather roll somewhat resembling a motorist's kit of tools. But the little instruments it contained were of more highly tempered steel, and the tiny drills gleamed with diamond points — it was in fact the most complete set of miniature burglar's tools that could be obtained, and had come into his possession from no less a person than Al Benthall, the Chicago bank-smasher.

The sonorous notes of Big Ben were booming out midnight when Lionel got out of a taxi opposite the County Hall, Westminster, and paying, the driver, swung off in the direction of Wharf Street.

A drizzle of rain was falling, and this had increased to a downpour by the time he had reached the big gates giving entrance to the warehouse owned by the Amalgamated Textile Company. There was not a soul about in the narrow street, and the only sound was the swish of the rain, the hiss and clank of a steam derrick somewhere along the riverbank, and the faint dismal hoot of a tug going down-stream.

Glancing swiftly about him, Crane bent down, and examined the padlock that fastened the gates. It was heavy and well constructed, and he concluded that it would take some time to pick, also there was the possibility of a patrolling policeman finding it unfastened while he was inside, and investigating the cause. On the whole it would be better to leave the thing intact, and gain entrance by some other means.

He looked up. The wooden gates were fairly high, but the stone buttresses from which they swung offered an easy foothold. With another quick look about him, Crane put his foot on one of the projecting hinges, and gripping the top of the gate hoisted himself up and astride. A moment later he had dropped lightly into the courtyard beyond.

So far, so good. The worst part of his task was over. Now he could work at his leisure, without risk of being seen. It was pitch dark, and to avoid stumbling over the mass of rubble that littered the place, he took out an electric torch and flashed it momentarily, to take stock of his surroundings. Above him to the right rose the huge bulk of the warehouse, and by the light of the lamp he was able to make out a narrow door in the brick wall, and towards this he made his way. The lock was a patent one, but he unrolled his kit of tools, and selecting a curiously shaped instrument, he began to work swiftly and surely on the small keyhole. At the end of ten minutes the door swung open under his pressure, and stepping into the darkness beyond, he closed it behind him and stood in the interior of the deserted building.

There was a slight scurrying sound, a patter of innumerable tiny feet as his entrance disturbed the army of rats that infest all such places, but otherwise dead silence. A beam of light cut through the darkness, as he flashed on his torch, and showed him that he was in a short narrow passage, that apparently led into the warehouse proper, and advancing along this he presently found himself in a large, lofty room, packed high with packing cases and various other lumber.

He quickly came to the conclusion that he was unlikely to find what he wanted here, and continued his exploration. A rough wooden staircase led upwards to a square hole in the ceiling, obviously giving admittance to the upper part of the building, and ignoring this for the time being, Crane concentrated his attention on a door at the opposite end of the room.

It was locked, but quickly yielded under the skilful manipulation of the instrument he had used before. Stepping across the threshold he fanned the light of the lamp over the small, office-like chamber beyond, and his eyes gleamed.

It was apparently a combination of office and living room, for a ramshackle and dusty desk was the main article of furniture, and over in one corner he made out the dim outline of a camp bed on which a number of rugs had been neatly folded. A plain deal table, and a chair completed the furnishing. This was a likely place for Kielmann to have chosen for the hiding place of incriminating documents. Crane began to make a close inspection of the place.

He was on his knees carefully searching the bare boards when suddenly he went rigid, his muscles tense, his ears straining to catch again the slight sound that had disturbed him. It came again, the click of a key in the lock, followed by the gentle closing of a door.

Somebody had entered the warehouse!

He switched off his torch, and waited in the blackness as the soft shuffling step drew nearer and nearer.

16

Kielmann's Secret

The footsteps paused, and Crane saw a momentary flash of light round the lintel of the half-closed door. There came the sound of some heavy object dropped on bare boards, and then the footsteps proceeded again. Crane drew in his breath with a sharp hiss as he suddenly realised that the newcomer was making for the office room — the room in which he was hiding at that moment.

Swiftly and noiselessly he acted. In two silent strides he had reached the camp bed, and dropping flat on the floor rolled himself beneath it. He was only just in time, for almost at the same moment he heard a muttered exclamation as the midnight visitant discovered the open door. There followed a short pause, and then with a slight click, as the switch was pressed down, the electric light in the centre of the room sprang into life. Peering out from under the bed, Crane saw a man standing on the threshold, and recognised the large, flabby face of Mr. Alexander Kielmann.

For a second or two the stout man stood there, shooting little, quick, darting, suspicious glances about the room, and then apparently satisfied with his scrutiny he entered leaving the door open. He was dressed in a heavy overcoat, and a muffler was wound round his neck. Slipping this off he flung it on the floor, mopping his face with a handkerchief. Obviously Mr. Kielmann had undergone a certain amount of physical exertion, thought Crane, and wondered what it was.

He was soon to learn, for having wiped his face and neck, the stout man replaced his handkerchief and went out, returning almost at once carrying a heavy leather suitcase which he dumped down in the middle of the room.

He seemed nervous and ill at ease, for he kept glancing behind him into the darkness of the storeroom with little quick jerks as though he expected someone to appear from the black void. He even went to the door to listen, although Crane, whose hearing was abnormal, had heard no sound. At last, having reassured himself that there was no unseen eavesdropper, he came back to the middle of the room, and searched in his pockets. Producing something that gleamed in the light, he next went over to the wall on the right hand side of the wall, and appeared to press hard at a spot on a level with his eyes.

With his pulses racing and his body tense, Crane watched him from his place of concealment. Was Kielmann himself going to show him the hiding place he had suspected and had come there to seek? It seemed so, for under the fat hand of the stout man, a portion of the wall opened outwards and in the space behind Crane saw the polished steel door of a safe!

Mr. Kielmann reached into the aperture, and there was the clicking rap of a combination dial being spun. Crane experienced a wave of excitement as a moment later he saw the heavy door of the wall safe pulled open.

The secret hiding place containing the documents and papers relating to Mr. Alexander Kielmann's nefarious business was a secret no longer, for even as Crane watched with straining eyes, the stout man brought forth bundle after bundle of papers and letters and placed them on the floor at his feet. They were all neatly tied together in separate packets, and when he had taken out the last, Mr. Kielmann closed the door of the safe, swung back the concealing portion of the wall, and proceeded to carry the safe's contents over to the table.

Pulling up a chair he seated himself, and began quickly but methodically to go through them.

Some he glanced at and tore up, others he laid on one side, working with a nervous energy that indicated his desire to be through with the whole business as quickly as possible.

There was now no longer any doubt, thought Crane, that he contemplated a getaway, and had come to destroy or take with him any evidence that might be discovered after he had gone. And here was the chance that the police had been hoping and waiting for, for years, and which even Crane himself had given up as hopeless — the chance of catching the elusive Mr. Kielmann with sufficient evidence in his possession to warrant an arrest.

He must never get away with the contents of that safe, and Crane swiftly made up his mind as to his course of action. Slipping his hand into the pocket of his coat, he pulled out an automatic and swung back the safety catch, and then with a sudden twist, wriggled from under the bed and sprang to his feet

'Good evening, Mr. Kielmann,' he said pleasantly, covering the stout man with his pistol. 'I see that business is keeping you up late. May I offer you my assistance in going through that formidable pile of papers you have before you?'

At the first sound of movement Kielmann had swung round with a squeal of fear, and his right hand flew to his hip pocket.

'Don't do that,' snapped Crane sharply.

'Keep your hands on the table.'

'Crane!' stammered the other, and there was relief as well as astonishment in his voice, and a tinge of colour crept back to his flabby cheeks.

Lionel nodded.

'Yes,' he remarked. 'For a second you were afraid it was the White Friar, weren't you, Kielmann? It's only me, less formidable perhaps, but equally persistent.'

'What are you doing here?' said Kielmann recovering himself. 'You have no right here at all.'

'Not the slightest,' admitted Lionel with a smile, 'but I'm very glad I came all the same.'

'What did you come for?' snarled the other. 'And how did you get in?'

'I broke in,' said Crane calmly. 'As to what I came for, Kielmann — well, I came to try and find those papers.'

Mr. Kielmann's mouth twitched, and a hunted expression crept into his beady eyes.

'They are nothing,' he muttered, 'merely — er — business documents connected with my companies. It is important that I should have a — er — lease first thing in the morning, so I came — '

'A liar you are, and a liar you always will be, Kielmann,' broke in Lionel without heat. 'I'm going to take those papers, and you to the nearest police station.'

'This is an outrage!' cried the stout man angrily, but his face had gone white. 'You have no right to meddle with my private property. You'll get yourself into serious trouble over this, I warn you.'

'I'm willing to take the risk,' retorted Crane, 'If I get into worse trouble over it than you do, I shall be surprised. Come on, Kielmann, put those papers together and give them to me. I'm afraid that airplane's going to wait a long time for you in the morning.'

Mr. Kielmann glared at him, and if looks could kill, Crane would have died on the spot there and then. He gave one wild glance towards the door as though contemplating making a dash for it, but Lionel shook his head warningly and waggled his pistol.

'I shouldn't try that, if I were you,' he advised, and without removing his eyes from the fat man strolled round and took up his position in front of the open doorway.

'I suppose you've got the whip-hand,' snarled Kielmann with an oath, 'But you're going to be sorry for this, I — '

He broke off, and Crane seeing the sudden look that flashed to his eyes, swung round, but he was too late. Even as he turned he received the full force of a shattering blow on the back of his head, caught an instantaneous glimpse of the triumphant face of the Frenchman, Maurice, and then his legs gave way beneath him, and he collapsed on the floor in a crumpled heap, and consciousness fled.

★　★　★

Crane's senses came back to him accompanied by a vivid pain in his head, and a dull rumble of sound that for some time he found it hard to place. Then suddenly it came to him. It was the subdued voices of two people in animated conversation. He opened his eyes and discovered that he was still in the office room, and an attempted movement also disclosed the fact that he had been securely trussed up and gagged.

The animated conversation was being carried on between Mr. Kielmann and the Frenchman, and as the mist cleared from Lionel's numbed brain, he began to distinguish a word here and there, and hearing, became interested. The point of the argument appeared to be connected with money, for the Frenchman was talking in a low, excited whisper that rose occasionally to a shrill whine as he became more emphatic.

'You 'ave much more money than me,' he was saying. 'Much more, and it ees only fair that you should divide it more equally.'

'I'm taking you with me in the plane, ain't I?' answered Kielmann. 'What more do you want?'

The Frenchman waved his hands excitedly.

'A lot more I want,' he said. 'I want more money, and I do not want to go with you on the plane. I prefer to stay 'ere in London.'

'Well, you can stay here, if you want to,' growled the stout man. 'But you won't get any more money, so you'd better stop arguing.'

'Oh, I won't, will I not?' retorted Maurice. 'We will see about that. Listen, I 'ave been a good and faithful friend to you — '

'Rubbish!' broke in Kielmann. 'Don't start that sentimental stuff with me. It won't cut any ice. You've been paid for everything you've done, and paid well. You've got nothing to grumble at.'

'But I am grumbling,' cried the other shrilly. 'You 'ave not, as you call it, played the fair game. There is more due to me, than I have got.'

'You'll get no more, so shut up!' snarled Kielmann angrily. 'If you don't want to come with me, you can go to blazes, but you won't get another penny. Is that plain enough?'

'It is plain, but I tell you — '

'Tell me nothing!' roared the stout man. 'Let's finish what we've got to do here, and get away.'

'Unless I get what I want,' said the Frenchman leaning across the table menacingly, 'I will do no more, and I warn you, if you do not give me my fair share of that money, I will go straight to the Scotland Yard.'

'Oh, you'll go straight to the Scotland Yard, will you?' said Kielmann softly, and Crane saw his teeth show in a mirthless grin. 'You'll squeal will you?'

'I will, unless you give me what is due to me.'

'All right,' the stout man's voice was suddenly very gentle. 'I'll give you what's due to you.'

'Good!' answered the other in a tone of satisfaction, 'then give it me now.'

Mr. Kielmann put a fat hand into his breast pocket, and then all at once his body grew tense, and an alert look sprang into his beady eyes.

The watchful Maurice saw it, and looked at his companion enquiringly.

'What is the matter?' he asked.

'Shut up!' hissed Kielmann softly.

'What the — '

'Shut up, I tell you!' The stout man leaned forward in a listening attitude, his eyes fixed on the partly open door.

Crane had heard nothing up to that moment, probably because his attention had been entirely concentrated on the two men at the table. But now he could distinguish a faint sound, which came from the storeroom. It was a creak, followed by another as though someone were stealthily crossing the bare boards.

Mr. Kielmann's hand came swiftly out of his pocket, and he held in his grasp a small but wicked-looking automatic.

Making a sign to the Frenchman to keep still, he tiptoed quickly and silently over to the door and stopped, listening again intently.

Again came the same sound, but now it sounded almost directly outside.

With a sudden bound forward Kielmann wrenched open the door, darted through, and the next moment Crane heard the sound of a sharp cry, followed by a heavy thud. The Frenchman became galvanised to action, at the noise, and with a muttered exclamation dashed through the open doorway. Lionel heard him give an exclamation of surprise, and then there was a muttered colloquy, which ended in a dragging sound as they reappeared hauling a limp form between them. This they dumped down in the middle of the room, and Crane started as he recognised the white, blood-stained face of Harry Pollard!

'He must have followed his precious friend,' panted Kielmann glaring down at the senseless form at his feet. 'Well, it's a bit of luck in a way. He can follow him on a longer and less pleasant journey.'

'Is he — dead?' asked Maurice in a low voice.

The stout man shook his head.

'No, not yet,' he answered grimly, 'I only stunned him with the butt of the pistol.'

He went over to the corner of the room, and came back with a length of rope. Bending down beside the unconscious Pollard, he began to tie him up securely whilst the Frenchman looked on wiping the perspiration from his forehead.

'What are you going to do with them?' he asked as Kielmann deftly gagged Pollard with his own handkerchief, and rose to his feet. 'You can't leave them here. They will be found and — '

'What little anybody can find of them, when I've finished, they'll be welcome to,' snarled the stout man. 'I'm taking no risks. Crane knows too much now, and I've no intention of leaving him in a position to tell what he knows.' He paused and then suddenly; 'There's a half-open case of celluloid boxes in the storeroom — just behind the door. Go and drag it in here.'

Maurice looked at him in surprise.

'Celluloid boxes?' he repeated. 'What do you want with celluloid boxes?'

'Don't talk so much,' grated Kielmann turning on him furiously. 'Do as you're told!'

For a moment the Frenchman looked rebellious and then with a shrug of his shoulders went out.

Kielmann examined his pistol for a moment, pressed down the safety catch, and slipped it into his pocket. Then he went over and stared down at Crane. Lionel kept his eyes half-closed. There was nothing to be gained by letting Kielmann know he had recovered consciousness, and there was a faint chance that if the stout man still believed him to be knocked out by the blow he had received, he might turn it to his own advantage. For a vague idea of why Kielmann wanted those celluloid boxes had flashed to his brain, and he felt dizzy with the horror of the possibility.

He heard the Frenchman stumbling about in the other room, and then a slithering, dragging sound as he began pulling a heavy packing case across the floor. Presently he appeared in the doorway breathless.

'I cannot get it any farther,' he panted, 'it's too big to come through the door.'

'It'll do where it is,' snapped Kielmann turning and going over to him. 'Help me take the boxes out.'

He went outside, followed by Maurice, and a handful of small white boxes of the type in which face cream is packed was thrown into the office room.

'Just bundle them out anyhow,' ordered Kielmann, 'and throw them in there.'

They worked quickly, and in less than five minutes, a large pile of the boxes occupied the centre of the room.

'There are no more,' said Maurice at last, and Kielmann came back and looked at the pile with satisfaction.

'We shan't want any more,' he said, and dragging the senseless body of Pollard beside Crane, he began arranging the boxes until they formed a circle with a shallow depression in the centre. 'There, that'll do,' he said straightening up, and went over to a small cupboard in the corner. 'I wonder if there are any left,' he went on, searching in the interior. 'Sutton used to keep a supply I know. Ah, here we are, the last one too.'

He returned with a candle and breaking it in half, picked up one of the celluloid boxes. By the aid of a match he melted the end of one half of the candle, and stuck it securely in the box. And then stooping, he placed it so that it stood in the middle of the pile of boxes.

'There,' he said with a flash of teeth triumphantly surveying his handiwork. 'All we have to do just before we go, is to light the candle, and when it burns down and reaches the box — pouff! The Amalgamated Textile Company's warehouse will go up in smoke and Mr. Lionel Crane and his clever partner with it.'

The Frenchman looked at his chief with horror-filled eyes, and Crane felt his flesh creep, and the perspiration break out on his forehead. It was a fiendish scheme and worthy of the man who had planned it.

'Mon Dieu! How horrible!' breathed Maurice.

'I think it's rather clever,' retorted Kielmann coolly shrugging his broad shoulders. 'However, time is getting on.' He glanced at his watch

'Before we go, you want me to give you what is due to you, don't you?'

The horror faded instantly from the other's eyes, and was replaced by an expression of cupidity.

'That is right,' replied Maurice eagerly. 'Let us settle up.'

'Let us settle up,' agreed Mr. Kielmann. 'Now if I — what was that?' he ended sharply and following the direction of his startled gaze the Frenchman turned round towards the door.

The deed occupied only a second — the crowning act of treachery to Mr. Alexander Kielmann's existence. A sharp report, and a little cloud of smoke, and the Frenchman spun round, and fell sprawling to the floor — dead before he even realised what had killed him.

With scarcely a glance at his erstwhile associate the stout man restored his still reeking pistol to his pocket, and picked up his overcoat, donning it leisurely as he might have done, had he been in his club. Looking round as though to assure himself that he had forgotten nothing, he picked up the box of matches he had used before, struck one and with a perfectly steady hand lighted the candle in the centre of the celluloid boxes. It spluttered for a moment and then began to burn steadily. Mr. Kielmann watched it for a moment with a smile, and then stooping he picked up his suitcase.

'I think that's all,' he said softly.

'Not quite all,' said a hollow voice, and with a smothered cry Kielmann faced the door.

Standing on the threshold was the figure — the long white robe, the white cowl and in the white gloved hand a menacing automatic pointing steadily at the stout man's heart.

'I am Death,' went on the eerie voice. 'To each of your friends I have come in turn as I said I would. You are the last, Kielmann, and now I have come for you!'

17

The Judgment of the White Friar

For a long while there was a dead silence broken only by the faint spluttering of the burning candle. The suitcase had fallen with a thud from Alexander Kielmann's nervous hand. He stood there motionless, facing his unknown enemy, his face a living advertisement of the fear in his heart. The figure in white regarded him silently, a veritable statue of doom. 'What — what do you want of me?' croaked Kielmann at length, and even to himself his voice sounded strange as though the words had been uttered by someone other than he.

'I want a life for a life,' was the answer. 'I want your life for the life of Len Sutton, which you took from him in this very room.'

'Who are you?' the question came like a sob in the throat.

'I have told you,' said the cowled man. 'I am Death, and I have been waiting for you for a long time, Kielmann. Who I really am you shall know — just before you die.'

The stout man shuddered.

'Is there nothing I can give you that will make you leave me alone?' he asked. 'I have a lot of money — in cash on me now. I will give it to you all, if you will only let me go.'

'Give it to Len Sutton,' said the other. 'Give it to André Maurice. Give it to the many people who have died as the result of your persecution, it will be of more use to them than to me. If you gave me all the money in the world, it would not be enough to turn me from my purpose.'

Kielmann passed his tongue across his dry lips, and looked wildly from one side to the other.

'What are you going to do with me?' he asked huskily. 'Surely you won't murder me in cold blood? You will at least give me a chance?'

'Did you ever give anyone a chance?' said the inexorable voice. 'Did you give

Len Sutton a chance?'

Kielmann plucked at his lower lip with a trembling hand.

'You keep on speaking about Sutton,' he whispered. 'What was Sutton to you?'

The white-garbed figure was silent for so long, that Mr. Kielmann repeated his question.

'What was Len Sutton to you?' he asked.

'He was my son,' answered the other, and for the first time his voice broke. 'My son whom you and your associates dragged to ruin.'

'Your son?' Kielmann staggered back as though from a physical blow, clutching the table for support. 'Merciful God — your son!'

'Now you know why it is useless to offer me bribes to let you go,' said the cowled man. 'Many weeks ago I swore that I would exterminate you one by one, leaving you until the last, and I have kept my word.'

'It was not I who ruined your son,' said Kielmann desperately. 'When Patricia York met him at Monte Carlo he was already a fugitive from justice — spending the money he had acquired by embezzlement.'

'Who made him a fugitive from justice?' was the reply. 'Who held over his head certain foolish letters that he had written while he was at Oxford, and demanded an outrageous sum for their return? Who threatened to send those letters to a man who shall be nameless unless that sum was paid? Who suggested, since he refused to go to his father for the money, a means by which it could be obtained? You did, Kielmann, or rather your agent, Beaumont, acting on your instructions did. He is beyond my vengeance, for he died eighteen months ago.'

'Then' — a look of wild terror sprang into Kielmann's eyes — 'your son's name was — Cecil Mortimer!'

The cowled man inclined his hooded head.

'But I never knew that Cecil Mortimer and Len Sutton were connected, I thought Mortimer — was dead,' stammered the stout man.

'Did you ever trouble to find out what had become of him?' said Charles Mortimer harshly. 'No, after you had dragged your pound of flesh out of him, he could go to perdition for all you cared. When Patricia York met him at Monte Carlo, he had changed his name to Len Sutton. Beaumont had done all the negotiating with Cecil Mortimer, and since none of you had ever seen him, and Beaumont was dead, why should you connect the prematurely aged Len Sutton with the man you had ruined? The woman, however, always on the lookout for fresh recruits for your vile gang saw in Len Sutton someone who might possibly be useful. She exercised all her fascination to bring him to heel, and soon had him completely under her thumb. She brought him back with her to London and introduced him to you. You used him to fake your books so that the Amalgamated Textile Company showed a bigger profit than it really made. You taught him to take drugs, and when finally he rebelled against the life of crime you were making him lead, you shot him like a mad dog.'

'How do you know all this?' muttered Kielmann.

'How do I know?' replied the other. 'Because on the night he died, I met him on Westminster Bridge, recognised him and arranged to come and see him on the following evening — here. I tried to persuade him to come with me then and there, but he wouldn't. He made an appointment for twelve o'clock, and said he would meet me at the gate. I kept that appointment, but Cecil wasn't there. The gate was open, however, and I crept in, and hearing voices inside the warehouse I explored further. Saw you and Dawson, Tison and Arnott talking in this room. There was blood upon the table, and you held in your hand a sheet of paper on which Cecil had drawn the picture of a White Friar. You were discussing the murder of poor Cecil and how you would dispose of the body, and said you had to kill him because he had decided to leave on the following day, and you were afraid that he might give you and your rotten associates away to the police. If I had any weapon on me then, you would all have been dead that night, but I hadn't, and you were too many for an old man to tackle empty-handed. I went away with the intention of going to the police, and then I thought of the scandal that would be dragged up around poor Cecil's name. And anyway they would only be able to hang you, and everyone of you were equally guilty. I went home and thought it over, and decided to take the law into my own hands. I would exact vengeance from you all, and I have, Kielmann. On every one — except you.'

The stout man had listened to Charles Mortimer's long speech in silence, still convulsively clutching the table, but now as he finished Crane saw his right hand move stealthily and slowly towards the pocket which contained the revolver he had used to kill the Frenchman. The cowled man had apparently been too intent on Kielmann to notice the bound figures of Crane and Pollard lying half hidden under the pile of celluloid boxes, or the candle, which was burning steadily down to the inflammable material that surrounded it.

'So you are Len Sutton's father,' said Kielmann. 'I guessed that you were some relation, but I never guessed the truth.'

His hand had almost reached the pocket.

'Well there's nothing I can say or do that will alter your determination I suppose?'

'Nothing,' said the other. 'There is no good reason why you should live, Kielmann, and many why you should die. You have exactly two minutes before you go to join your friends, before you solve the greatest secret of all.'

'If I solve it, you shall solve it with me!' snarled Kielmann and his hand flashed to his pocket.

The pistol in the other's hand cracked viciously, but the stout man ducked and the bullet lodged harmlessly in the opposite wall. Before Charles Mortimer could fire again, Kielmann had leaped at him and wrenched the long-barrelled automatic from his grasp. It fell with a clatter to the bare floor, and as he jerked out his own pistol, Charles Mortimer gripped his wrists and deflected the muzzle.

Crack! Crack!

Kielmann fired desperately, but the bullets buried themselves in the floor, and then with a sharp twist the cowled man numbed the muscles of his arm, and the weapon flew out of his hand. The next instant they had closed, and each striving his hardest for supremacy, went staggering back and forth across the room. Kielmann possessed abnormal strength for so stout a man, and undoubtedly would have easily overcome his adversary, if at the crucial moment his foot had not slipped on the other half of the candle, which when he had staggered against the table had rolled to the floor. It upset his balance, and still clutching his opponent he fell heavily — into the midst of the pile of celluloid boxes. His fall overturned the lighted candle, and immediately a white-hot sheet of flame roared ceilingwards. The sudden intense heat singed Crane's eye-brows, and the white flame blinded him. With a prodigious effort he rolled away from that seething inferno, in the midst of which the two closely locked figures still struggled madly, and with his clothes alight in a dozen places, waited for the end from which it seemed nothing could now save them!

18

The End of the Story

The heat was terrific, and the pungent fumes of the burning celluloid, mingling with the dense volumes of smoke made breathing an agony. With smarting eyes and choked lungs Lionel Crane tried desperately to free himself, for the fire had taken hold so rapidly that it was now only a question of moments before the whole building became a raging furnace. His bonds, however, refused to give an inch, and by the irony of fate those parts of his clothing that were smouldering, had not come in contact with the cords at his wrist and ankles.

Pollard was still unconscious, and Crane hoped that he would continue so until the end. It would be more merciful that way. The other two figures almost hidden now in the white heart of the holocaust lay still, either from the effects of the flames and fumes, or else as the result of that last fierce fight which had precipitated the fire.

Crane's skin was scorched in a dozen places and he felt his brain swimming — great clouds of darkness swept across his senses blotting out momentarily the blazing light of the hungry fire as it crackled and roared with fiendish glee at every fresh hold gained. This, then, was the finish. Strange, fantastic pictures flitted before his eyes — little almost forgotten memories of his youth — the half-timbered front of an old inn where he had spent a holiday — a collection of unrelated and irrelevant episodes that chased across his brain like constantly moving pictures on a cinema screen. He felt himself floating as it seemed, and it was a curiously gratifying sensation that was marred by an acute pain that appeared to envelop his whole body and yet was something apart from himself. He became obsessed with the ridiculous notion that he was in a hot bath, and that someone was filling it against his will with boiling, scalding water. He tried to pierce the clouds of steam that rose around him, in an endeavour to see who was responsible for this — made out the vague outline of a face without a body that hovered in mid-air — and recognised without the slightest feeling of surprise, the face of Dick Venner. The face loomed nearer — grew to gigantic proportions — and then suddenly seemed to explode in a flash of light —

*   *   *

'He'll do now. He's pretty badly scorched, I but it's nothing serious.'

The words came faintly as from a long distance, and Crane opened his eyes.

Two people were bending over him, a stranger and Dick Venner. So it hadn't been an hallucination. Venner had been responsible for that infernal hot water. His whole body was stiff and sore, and he made up his mind to say a few forceful words to the young man regarding his foolish trick. How in the world had he got into the bathroom anyway?

'He's recovering consciousness.' It was

the stranger who spoke, and behind him Crane saw another figure — the white-clad form of a nurse.

A nurse! Where the deuce was he, and what had happened? He tried to move an arm and found that he couldn't. It was heavy like lead, and seemed strangely large. He looked down and saw that both his arms and hands were swathed in bandages. Extraordinary! He was lying on a bed.

'You were only just in time, Mr. Venner.' It was the strange voice speaking again. 'Another two or three minutes and they would both have been burned to death.'

Burned to death? That was it. There had been a fire. He remembered the smoke and the reek — the pungent odour of celluloid. Like a flash the enveloping mist rolled from his brain. The office room in the warehouse at Lambeth . . . the locked figures fighting desperately in their last terrible embrace . . . the fierce white-hot greedy flames . . .

'Where am I?' His voice was husky and so weak that it scarcely rose above a whisper as he tried unsuccessfully to sit up.

'You're all right, Mr. Crane,' said the stranger in a soothing tone bending over him. 'You're in Westminster Hospital. Your friend, Mr. Venner, brought you here. He rescued you from the fire just in time.'

A sudden thought came to Lionel.

'What about Pollard?' he asked. 'Is he safe?'

'Quite,' smiled the doctor. 'He's in the next bed.'

'Hello, Li,' greeted a faint but cheery voice, and with an effort Crane turned his head in the direction from whence it came.

Harry Pollard, his face almost entirely concealed in bandages, was lying in a narrow bed a few feet away.

'I don't know what the date is,' he said with an attempt at a grin, 'but I feel that it ought to be the fifth of November.'

Crane tried to smile back, felt the skin crack about his mouth, and still trying to smile, relapsed once more into unconsciousness . . .

* * *

It was twelve o'clock on the following day, and feeling much better except for the throbbing pain of his burns, Crane was sitting up in bed talking to Dick Venner who was perched on the foot.

Pollard, who had suffered less than Lionel from the effect of the holocaust, was consuming black grapes at an alarming rate, devoting his attention more or less equally between the succulent fruit and the conversation that was taking place between his partner and his visitor.

'The whole building was gutted,' said Dick, 'and the firemen had a dickens of a job to save the two factories adjoining. By the time I had got you two out and given the alarm the fire had got such a hold that there was no possibility of coping with it.'

'The bodies of Kielmann and your uncle were not found?' asked Lionel.

Dick shook his head.

'No they must have been burned under the debris when the top part of the building fell in,' he answered. 'They were both dead when I arrived.'

'How did you get there so opportunely?' said Crane after a slight pause.

'I followed my uncle,' was the reply, and Lionel nodded, and instantly winced at the pain the movement caused.

'Of course, you knew,' he murmured softly, and again Dick nodded.

'Yes, I knew,' he answered. 'I knew from the time I ran into him at Horsham after he had killed Tison. He told me the whole story that evening, just before you and Herrick came to arrest me.'

'And it was he, of course, who dropped your handkerchief?' Lionel went on.

'Yes, his own hadn't come home from the laundry, and he borrowed mine earlier in the day,' said Dick. 'I tried my hardest to make him give up his scheme of vengeance — but he wouldn't, and — Well I couldn't very well give my own uncle away could I, and besides to a certain extent, I sympathised with him.'

'He was a murderer,' said Crane.

'Was he?' Dick pursed his lips. 'One isn't a murderer if one exterminates vermin!'

'Nothing can justify the taking of human life,' replied Lionel though he felt that the sentence was a trifle sententious. 'However, he is beyond punishment. By the way, what happened to Miss Rayland? Of course, your uncle found her on the night Dawson took her to the warehouse. What did he do with her?'

Dick smiled.

'He brought her back home,' he replied. 'The shock had made her terribly ill, and she had recognised Uncle Charles, so we were afraid to take her to her own home, in case in her weak condition she gave uncle away'

'I see,' said Crane. 'I suppose she's still there.'

'Yes, I think she'll be well enough to get up in a few days.'

'And then there'll be a wedding,' broke in Pollard. 'Well, don't forget me — I like cake.'

Dick reddened.

'You shall have a special one, all to yourself,' he retorted.

There was a short silence, and then Crane said suddenly:

'Did your uncle know Sir James Lavendale?'

'Very well indeed,' replied Dick in surprise. 'They were the closest friends. Why?'

'Only that it accounts for two things,' answered Lionel. 'Sir James has a flat opposite Kielmann's, and he has been away for some time. Your uncle must have had a key, for undoubtedly Arnott was lured to that flat and killed there. The trunk was either already there, or taken in some days previously. It was a simple matter to carry it just across the landing, and leave it outside Kielmann's door. Also on the day Morley was shot in my presence, Sir James' flat formed an ideal hiding place. Your uncle had only to take off his white robe, and slip across to the flat, and wait until the coast was clear. When the porter and I came up by the lift, he must have seized his opportunity and gone down by the stairs.'

Again there was a silence, which was broken by Crane.

'I suppose you know,' he said, 'that you can be arrested as an accessory?'

'Yes, I know that.' The young man looked gloomy.

'Have you made any statement to the police?' asked Crane.

'No, not yet.'

'It seems to me unnecessary to rake up a scandal which can do nobody any good,' Lionel went on thoughtfully. 'After all, I don't hold an official position. If I did it would be different.'

'You mean — ' exclaimed Dick eagerly.

'I mean,' answered Lionel Crane, 'suppose we leave it as it is? Charles Mortimer is dead — he cannot be punished by an earthly court. His son is dead, Kielmann is dead. Let the mystery of the White Friar remain a mystery and die, too.'

'Mr. Crane, you're a brick!' cried Dick Venner his eyes gleaming, and Lionel smiled.

'That's exactly what I feel like,' he said humorously. 'A brick that has just come out of the furnace!'

THE END

We do hope that you have enjoyed reading this large print book.

Did you know that all of our titles are available for purchase?

We publish a wide range of high quality large print books including:
Romances, Mysteries, Classics
General Fiction
Non Fiction and Westerns

Special interest titles available in large print are:
The Little Oxford Dictionary
Music Book, Song Book
Hymn Book, Service Book

Also available from us courtesy of Oxford University Press:
Young Readers' Dictionary
(large print edition)
Young Readers' Thesaurus
(large print edition)

For further information or a free brochure, please contact us at:
Ulverscroft Large Print Books Ltd.,
The Green, Bradgate Road, Anstey,
Leicester, LE7 7FU, England.
Tel: (00 44) **0116 236 4325**
Fax: (00 44) **0116 234 0205**

Other titles in the
Linford Mystery Library:

THE WOLVES OF CRAYWOOD

V. J. Banis

Dark tragedy strikes the three Cray brothers: two girls have been brutally torn apart by vicious beasts — the countryside around Craywood blazes with the legends of the were wolf. No one believes that a man could have caused such horror . . . Gaye reluctantly answers her sister Susan's call for help and learns that Susan blames Walter Cray for the killings. Nightmare follows nightmare, and soon Gaye herself is marked for death! Can anyone stop *The Wolves of Craywood*?

TOMORROW, UTOPIA

Steve Hayes and David Whitehead

In Washington a high-ranking politician is murdered, whilst in Central Africa, a new virus is killing thousands of male victims. And on the internet, a group known as The Utopians grows in power. Is there a connection between all these things? Homicide Detective Ben Hicks, however, has his own problems. Meanwhile, Pentagon cryptologist Hunter McCormack witnesses the murder of a politician. Now the killers are out to silence her ... and no one believes she saw the killing. Except Ben ...

THE PLOT AGAINST SHERLOCK HOLMES

Gary Lovisi

When Sherlock Holmes finds himself enmeshed in the most deadly case of his career, it threatens to bring terrible doom upon him and his friend Doctor John H. Watson. A deadly nemesis from his past, a most vile and evil villain, has returned to England to wreak his revenge for past deeds. He unleashes a dastardly plot, which begins with a shocking murder in Whitechapel and causes Inspector Lestrade to believe that Jack the Ripper has returned . . .

CLOSELY KNIT IN SCARLATT

Ardath Mayhar

Olive, 'The Knit Lady,' is an unlikely secret agent. A professional assassin and in her sixties, she had been quietly recruited by 'The Brokers.' Now she is hired to kidnap and kill retired British agent Benjamin Scarlatt, but Olive has scruples. And when an Islamic terrorist group takes over the cruise ship on which both she and Scarlatt are travelling, she fights back with knitting needle, scalpel and plastic explosives — proving that it's dangerous to underestimate Little Old Ladies!

MURDER, MYSTERY AND MAGIC

John Burke

An innocent man is arrested for a murder committed by a woman . . . A guilty man confesses to another murder — but the police arrest an innocent woman! A man finds the woman of his dreams — and finds he's in a nightmare . . . The tenants of a new block of flats are so delighted with their new home that they don't really want to go out — little realizing that they *can't* leave. Strange incidents from macabre stories of *Murder, Mystery . . . and Magic*.